# AN ORCHID TO DIE FOR

K.C. AMES

17th
STREET
BOOKS

## LET'S CONNECT

Sign up to my newsletter and stay in touch (subscribers get my Costa Rican recipe book, for free!

kcames.com/subscribe

# CHAPTER ONE

Bagels, Books, and Lattes bustled as usual with caffeine-seeking patrons. It was exciting to see the business bustling, but Dana Kirkpatrick had to remind herself that it was the bagels and lattes side that was bustling. The book side, not so much.

It had been six months since Mindy and Leo Salas moved their successful cafe into Dana's bookstore located in the heart of Ark Row—the merchant district of Mariposa Beach—after their greedy landlord tripled the rent. There was limited retail space available in tiny Mariposa Beach, so the landlord figured Mindy and Leo wouldn't have much option but to pay up. He hadn't counted that Dana's bookstore had more room than she had books to fill it with, so she invited her friend to move her cafe into the bookstore.

Rent would be the same, and she wouldn't take a cut of their business. It was basically two businesses under one roof.

Dana was happy that they agreed. She was enjoying being a landlord, but she couldn't help but feel a tinge of envy at how busy Mindy's business was doing compared to the tepid business the bookstore was doing.

Dana wasn't born yesterday. She knew about the perils of opening a brick and mortar bookstore in the digital world. But she loved books and the book business; she just hoped business was better. She was still having fun with her bookstore, and the increase in traffic from Mindy's cafe was a blessing. Plenty of times one of Mindy's customers would wander over to the bookstore and buy a book while they waited for their caramel macchiato and their made-from-scratch bagels spread with one of Mindy and Leo's also made-from-scratch cream cheese with a tropic twist like mango and pineapple.

*Vanquish that green monster*, Dana told herself when she would throw an internal pity party for herself. The busy cafe also gave her the chance to get busy when the coffee shop got slammed with the morning and mid-afternoon rush. When that daily occurrence happened, Dana would jump over to the coffee side to pitch in.

It kept her busy, and she enjoyed being busy. It made the day go by so much faster than sitting on her side of the business, staring at the front door. It was also a bonus that she was working side-by-side with her friend.

ON THAT DAY, Dana sat behind the counter of her bookstore when she realized she had been daydreaming for about ten minutes. She looked around to make sure no one noticed she had been in la-la land. It was ten thirty a.m., the slow time between the breakfast and lunch rushes.

Amalfi Soto was restocking a book. She smiled when she made eye contact with Dana. Dana blushed, figuring she knew she was off in a daydream world.

Amalfi officially was Dana's bookstore employee, but she was spending more time working in the cafe. She had become quite the skilled barista, and Mindy needed more help than Dana did with customers, so she didn't mind.

"Excuse me, miss." It took Dana a moment to get out of her trance and realize that someone was talking to her.

She snapped out of her stupor and blushed, looking up at the man on the other side of her sales counter. She had the feeling he had been trying to get her attention before then.

"So sorry. I zoned out," Dana said, standing up from the chair.

"Looked that way," he said, smiling.

Dana felt embarrassed again. "How may I help you?"

He was an American in his late twenties. Blond. Tanned, but it didn't look like a tourist tan to Dana, more like a working outdoors type of tan. What they called a farmer's tan.

The man didn't dress like the typical tourist either. Those visitors usually wore thin T-shirts, swim trunks, and flip-flops. He wore a buttoned-up short-sleeve tan shirt, heavy-clothed cargo shorts, and Carhartt outdoor shoes.

His attire reminded Dana of Steve Irwin, the Crocodile Hunter. She figured he was headed out for a rugged outdoor adventure up in the mountain jungle. In Mariposa Beach alone there were three businesses dedicated to providing tourists with off-the-beaten-path tours up in the mountains.

It was the beauty of Costa Rica's Guanacaste Province where Mariposa Beach was located. You could lounge on the white-sand beach or go on a jungle trek all on the same day.

"Are you going hiking or four-wheeling?" Dana asked him.

He seemed confused but caught on after taking a quick glance at his attire.

He laughed. "No, I wish, that sounds like fun. I'm working today. Over at the wildflower reserve," he explained.

Dana lit up. "Oh, the one up by Loma Linda?"

The man nodded. "That's the one."

She had been meaning to visit the reserve ever since she moved down to Costa Rica.

"I've heard it's beautiful there. I've been living here for six months but haven't made it up there yet. It's on my to-do list."

"You should come on up. I'd be happy to give you a personal tour. My name is Max Perry," he said, holding out his hand in the air.

Dana shook it. "I'm Dana Kirkpatrick.

"So where are you from, Max?"

"I'm from Connecticut, how about yourself?"

"San Francisco. So how does a Connecticut Yankee end up working at a wildflower refuge in Costa Rica?"

He smiled. "I'm working on my Ph.D. specializing on tropical botany and conservation from the University of Hawaii. They have an exchange program with the reserve out here, so I applied and was happy to be selected. I've been here for two weeks so far."

"How cool. I love Hawaii, by the way. I used to go there every other year or so in another life," Dana said, smiling.

"I'm amazed how similar the Guanacaste Province is to Hawaii."

Dana nodded in agreement. She had noticed that as well.

"Which island is the university at?"

"Oahu."

"Oh, I thought botany school would be on one of the more remote islands," Dana said.

"It would surprise you. The university is located near the Mānoa Valley, where you would be hard-pressed to believe that you're only a few miles away from downtown Honolulu."

"Fascinating. Sorry to talk your ear off, how may I help you?"

"Well, I know it's a stretch, but I was wondering if you carry any local books about botany?"

"No, sorry, I gear my inventory towards beach reads for tourists. Not sure where you could even find local botany books around here. I would imagine you would need to go up to the city for that or from Amazon. Although the shipping down to Mariposa Beach might cost more than the actual book," Dana said. "I do carry a few bird-watching books since I had tourists asking for them, but that's as close to nature I have book-wise. Not counting a Nevada Barr mystery."

Max smiled. Dana thought he was a good-looking kid, and since he worked outdoors studying tropical flowers, it made sense why he had that farmer's tan going and why he looked like a zookeeper instead of a beach-lounging tourist.

An obnoxious customer who bellowed at Mindy on the cafe side interrupted Dana's pleasant conversation.

"How can it take this long to get my order?" the man cawed obnoxiously.

Both Dana and Max turned to look at the rude man.

"Sir, I explained we were out of mango cream cheese. We make our cream cheeses from scratch. Sometimes we run out, and I can't just whip some up just like that, but we still have regular cream cheese, strawberry, and jalapeño ready to go, and they're just as delicious," Mindy explained, sounding exasperated.

"I want the mango cream cheese," he said, sounding whiny.

"Then you're going to have to come back tomorrow morning," Leo Salas said, coming out from the kitchen glaring at the man that was being rude to his wife.

Leo Salas worked the kitchen. Dealing with rude customers was a delicate balance he knew well. Both Leo and Mindy had worked in the food industry for over a decade, including at fancy New York City restaurants, so they were used to dealing with New York-grade rude customers and snobby diners, but this guy was on a whole other level on the borderline of inappropriateness, so Dana wasn't surprised that Leo stepped out from the kitchen to chide the man.

Dana and Max shrugged their shoulders.

"Seems like a pleasant man," Max said, grinning.

"We get those from time to time," Dana said.

"Well, okay, thanks for your help. I do like a good crime thriller, so I'll check out what you have back there," Max said as he wandered off to the crime fiction section of the bookstore.

"Fine, I'll have the regular cream cheese then," the man barked as Dana watched Max heading over to the Mystery, Suspense, and Thriller section.

The rude man stomped over to the bookstore side.

*Great*, Dana thought.

He perused the books while constantly checking his phone. He looked at the book selection and hissed.

He gave Dana a side glance and said, "Bunch of crap you have here."

*Whoa*, Dana thought. This guy was really a piece of work. But she said nothing. Just ignored him. She had found it was the best way to deal with bullies like him.

"Have some manners, man," Max Perry scolded him from the crime fiction bookshelf. The man glanced back there and ignored him, focusing back on his iPhone.

After a couple minutes, Max Perry brought up a book by Nevada Barr. It was from her wonderful Anna Pigeon series of mystery novels set in national parks of the United States.

"You convinced me on Nevada Barr," Max said, putting the paperback on the sales counter. "I thought about becoming a park ranger before I got into botany research."

"You'll love it." Dana smiled and rang him up.

"Botany research?" the rude man asked as he walked up towards Max.

He got in close, making direct eye contact that made Dana back up, and she wasn't even the recipient of his attention.

Max stared back with a look of half curiosity and annoyance.

"Yes, I'm a botanist," he said.

"Are you a scientist?"

"I'm a plant biologist working on my Ph.D.. Why do you ask?"

"Are you one of the students at the wildflower reserve?" the rude man asked, ignoring his question. His voice had changed from being curt and rude to sounding interested in Max Perry. Like he had blipped on his radar of interest.

Both Dana and Max looked at the man with curiosity.

He was short and stocky, with a round, ruddy face. He wore a very busy Affliction shirt, navy blue shorts, and blue loafers on his sockless feet. *The man has a sense for color and flare in his douchey choice of clothing*, Dana thought.

"Yes. Have you been to the reserve?" Max asked.

"Your wheat bagel with regular cream cheese is ready," Mindy called out, interrupting them.

"Finally," the man huffed as he walked away from the counter where Max was standing at without answering that question either or even acknowledging him. He picked up his bagel and left, saying nothing else to anyone. Not even a thank you to Mindy.

"Strange man," Max said as he paid Dana for the book.

Dana shrugged. "I've seen stranger."

Max chuckled. "I can imagine working with the public you must get all types of people coming through those doors."

"Yes, indeed," Dana replied, giving Max change back.

"It's one of the reasons I enjoy working out on the field with my flowers. Although I have to do a lot of grant-money groveling."

"I'm afraid there is no way around having to interact with people from time to time," Dana said as she handed him the book he purchased.

"I was serious about my offer for a private tour of the reserve," Max said, jotting down his phone number on a piece of notebook paper which he tore out and handed to Dana.

"Thank you, I'll take you up on your offer. Is it okay if I bring my boyfriend?"

Dana said that because she knew Benny Campos would love it, and she didn't want to send a wrong message to the good-looking botanist.

If he seemed disappointed, he hid it well.

"Certainly, the more the merrier," he said, smiling wide.

# CHAPTER TWO

Things got quiet after the rude man left. Dana walked over to Mindy.

"What a tool, that guy," she said.

"It never ceases to amaze me how bent out of shape people can get over the silliest of things, like running out of mango cream cheese. Jeez. You'd think he was going into anaphylactic shock and I was lollygagging with the epinephrine injection."

Dana laughed. "Yeah, I would hate to see him dealing with actual serious problems in life. Did you hear him complain about my book selection?" Dana asked, rolling her eyes.

"No, I tuned him out as soon as he was out of my line of sight. I put a rush on his order so he would leave, but I'm not surprised he was rude to you too."

"He wasn't impressed with my book inventory."

"Mr. Sunshine," Mindy said.

"My customer barked at him when he got lippy with me," Dana said.

"I did notice him. Cute," she whispered the "cute" part.

They were both in their late thirties in happy relationships, and Mindy had been married for years, but they both giggled like school girls about the cute boy walking down the school hallway.

"So what's his story?" Mindy asked, smiling.

"He's a very interesting person, a botanist working on his Ph.D.. He's part of an exchange program working on a special project at the wildflower reserve."

"Doña Elsa Calderón's place?" Mindy asked.

"Yes. I've been meaning to visit there but haven't made it over there yet," Dana said.

"I haven't been there in years, but it's beautiful. She has a breathtaking array of orchids that are amazing to see in person."

"The botanist invited me and Benny for a personal tour."

"Take him up on it, you won't regret it. So what's a botanist anyway? Is that a fancy word for gardener?" Leo Salas asked, butting into the conversation from the kitchen.

Dana and Mindy laughed. "Not exactly. Botany is the scientific study of plants," Dana said.

"He's a scientist, hon, not a gardener," Mindy added.

"Plant scientist?" Leo asked, not sounding impressed.

"It's an important field, Leo. Plant biologists improve our supply of medicines, foods, plant products, they manage parks, forests, and help solve pollution problems," Dana explained.

"Huh, interesting," Leo said, shrugging his shoulders and stepping back into the kitchen.

"How long has that reserve been here?" Dana asked Mindy.

"I don't know, a long time. Two or three decades at least."

"It's not far, is it?" Dana asked.

"Nothing is too far around these parts. About fifteen miles from town, but Doña Elsa doesn't come down here much. I guess she's devoted to the reserve and spends all her time, day and night, at the reserve. She's highly respected in the municipality, but I hear she's a bit on the self-righteous side when it comes to protecting the wilderness, which is great, don't get me wrong, but I think you can do that without shaming and judging people."

"I would imagine she's seen a lot over the years that makes her feel that way about the subject matter," Dana said.

"Oh, she's seen a lot all right, but it has nothing to do with saving the forest," Doña Amada said, startling Dana and Mindy, who hadn't noticed her walk in.

"Hi, Doña Amada, didn't see you there," Dana said, grinning at the old lady.

Doña Amada was the de facto leader of the town's so-called Gossip Brigade, a group of four old ladies and life-long frenemies who liked to play canasta, gossip, and bicker with each other.

"So why is Doña Elsa a piece of work? Do tell," Mindy said, egging her on.

"That no-good husband of hers. That's why. He's a real lout that one. Why she puts up with his philandering and shenanigans is beside me," Doña Amada said.

She then placed her usual late-morning order with Mindy: piping hot coffee, black, and a pineapple empanada.

"I want it hot like that lady at McDonalds," Dana would hear her say to Mindy at least once a week when ordering her coffee.

"Oh, Doña Amada, you shouldn't say such things about people," Mindy said.

"It's the truth. Sometimes the truth hurts," Doña Amada replied self-assuredly.

"How do you know that about her husband and their private lives?" Dana asked.

Doña Amada laughed. "Everyone knows. You've been living here long enough now, dear, to know that this is a small community and we all know everything about everyone. There are no secrets in a small town," Doña Amada said, still laughing.

She sent a shiver down Dana's spine thinking that the whole town would know about her private business.

Doña Amada went on. "Her husband has been a no-good, double-timing shyster since he was knee high."

Amalfi Soto handed Doña Amada her coffee and empanada. "He hit on me once," Amalfi said casually.

"What?" Dana and Mindy said in unison, shocked.

"See what I tell you? He's a no-good lout," Doña Amada said, sounding vindicated.

"When was that?" Mindy asked.

"A few years ago when I was working at the resort. He was there at the bar and had put back a few rum and cokes. He made a few passes, I politely declined. Then as he left he patted my butt."

"Oh, gross! What a pig," Dana said.

"What did you do?" Mindy asked.

"Mr. Barca has strict rules of not making the customers feel uncomfortable, so I shrugged it off and left without saying anything to him, then I told my supervisor I wouldn't get near him again, so I stayed away when he was at the resort after that."

It wasn't surprising to Dana that Gustavo Barca, the owner of the five-star luxury resort nearby, Tranquil Bay, would allow guests and visitors to the resort to get away with such disgusting behavior against his staff.

His reputation for being a ruthless developer and hotelier was well earned, as Dana had learned when he tried to wrestle her Casa Verde property from her when she had first moved to Mariposa Beach from San Francisco to claim her inheritance.

Her moving to Mariposa Beach didn't align with the greedy developer's plans, so he offered to buy her property so he could bulldoze the beautiful beach house her uncle had built so he could build more luxury cabanas closer to the white sand beach in town.

"That's terrible," Dana said.

"It happened more than you could imagine working in the hotel business, especially one like Tranquil Bay Resort that caters to rich, powerful, entitled men," Amalfi said.

"Told you, a no-good lout," Doña Amada said once again.

"If he's hanging out at the resort, he must be rich," Dana said.

Doña Amada guffawed loudly. "He likes to play the part of the rich playboy, thinking he's suave like George Hamilton."

Inside, Dana laughed at the octogenarian's go-to for a suave, debonair type: George Hamilton. She wondered if he was still alive.

Doña Amada continued, "He doesn't have two dimes to his name, but he plays the part and he's always scheming with get-rich-quick plans and he loves to put on airs," she said as she grabbed her bag with her pineapple empanada and her to-go cup of coffee. She turned and began to scamper outside. "A lout," she said once again as the door closed behind her.

Dana, Mindy, and Amalfi laughed.

"She's not lying," Amalfi said.

"I hope I don't have to run into him when I visit the reserve," Dana said indignantly.

"Don't let him spoil the visit. When are you going?" Mindy asked.

"Benny is coming to town tonight, so I'll see if he's up to go up there on Saturday or Sunday. Of course, I'll need to check with Max to see if that works for him," Dana said.

## CHAPTER THREE

BENNY CAMPOS WAS DANA'S BOYFRIEND. THE LAST THING she was looking for when she moved to Costa Rica was a relationship. She thought her divorce had soured her from trying again for a long time—if not ever—until she met Benny.

He was an attorney who lived in Escazú, a suburb of San José, the capital and largest city of Costa Rica. He was Dana's lawyer handling the inheritance of her uncle's property and the legal entanglements that came with it.

They quickly became good friends, and slowly their relationship blossomed into more than just friendship. Both of them were divorcees, so neither of them were too eager to rush into a relationship, so they took things slow. *Slow as molasses*, as Dana's best friend in San Francisco, Courtney Lowe, liked to tease her.

Benny arrived at Casa Verde at seven o'clock p.m. and he brought a bowl of his homemade ceviche, which was one of Dana's favorite Costa Rican dishes. It was a simple dish that consists of corvina fish cut into cubes that is mixed with onions, red bell peppers, and jalapeños. Lemon juice and a splash of ginger ale is added to the bowl and then it's marinated a few hours in the refrigerator. The lemon juice cooks the fish. The dish is served chilled and it's delicious.

Dana had eaten plenty of ceviche before Costa Rica but was surprised that Benny would put ginger ale in there. He swore that the ginger ale was the secret ingredient that made regular ceviche a tico Ceviche.

He kissed Dana on his way to the kitchen. He put the bowl on the kitchen island and removed the plastic wrap as Dana went to her cupboard for the soda crackers and Salsa Lizano hot sauce, which were the perfect accompaniments for the dish.

Benny smiled. "You're eating ceviche like a local now."

She smiled sheepishly as she went to the fridge to get a couple of bottles of ice-cold Imperial beer.

"Yep, that confirms it, you're a tica," Benny teased.

They ate and talked about their week apart. It was the one part of the relationship that Dana found tough, the distance that was even more daunting in a new blossoming relationship when you then had to spend a week apart. But then again, maybe that was the secret to making it work.

Benny's home and law practice were located in the capital, 150 miles from Mariposa Beach, so the distance was a reality they had to contend with, especially since he also had a ten-year-old daughter that lived with her mother, making it difficult to spend as much time with her in Mariposa Beach. But she didn't want to think about that just then. She wanted to enjoy spending time with Benny drinking Costa Rican beer and eating ceviche tico style.

After a few bites, she remembered about Max Perry.

"Oh, guess what," she said excitedly. She could tell by his facial reaction that she had piqued his curiosity.

She told him about meeting Max Perry earlier in the day and how they had a standing invitation for a personalized tour of the wildflower reserve.

"I haven't been up there since I was a teenager," Benny said.

Although Benny was born and raised in the capital city, his family had a beach house located in Mariposa Beach since he was a child, so he spent a lot of his life in the Guanacaste Province.

"So you know Doña Elsa?"

"I do. She was born and raised in the Guanacaste Province. A woman of simple means. She started a small plant nursery in Loma Linda on property that had belonged to her family since the nineteenth century. Property that they had come into possession via squatter laws after her ancestors had lived on the land uncontested for decades, until eventually they legally came to own it. She was an only daughter and her parents passed away a long time ago, so all that land passed on to her."

"Oh my, squatters," Dana said.

"Well, not like you might think. No one owned that land in the nineteenth century. It's way up in the mountains. It's rough terrain. Her great-grandfather settled there. And eventually through hard work they turned it into a nice farm that provided for the family. In the nineteen seventies, the land had become more valuable and developers wanted to claim it. But considering it had been in Doña Elsa's family almost one hundred years, the courts made it official, giving her family the land."

"Sounds fair to me," Dana said.

"Agreed. When she started the small plant nursery, she discovered she was a real natural at it, and it became a thriving nursery. Eventually the plant nursery turned into the reserve, which she started on her own. She had no experience on how to operate a nature reserve, but she saw the encroachment of developers coming, so she took action, learning on her own and figuring out how to work with the municipality and national government powers that be to designate that piece of land as a wildlife and nature reserve to protect it from development. Her land is now worth millions of dollars, and she runs her nonprofit reserve protecting the land and the wildflowers that grow there. Some of her orchids are only found on her land. I'm happy to donate to her organization every now and then. She does good work."

"She sounds like an amazing woman. I heard her husband isn't as amazing," Dana said, sounding sheepish.

Benny looked at her askew. "Let me guess, the Gossip Brigade?"

Dana smiled. "Of course. Doña Amada was in the store when we were talking about the reserve, so she was more than happy to let us know about Doña Elsa's deadbeat, cheating husband."

"No doubt she relished filling you in on that," Benny said.

"The woman likes to gossip, what can I say."

"Well, I don't know anything personal about Doña Elsa and her husband Eladio, but yes, as far as the rumors are concerned, he doesn't have the most sterling of reputations as a husband or as a businessperson. I do recall he got into some financial problems a few years ago when one of his crazy business ideas failed. He also has a reputation of not paying his bills, so let's just say that I would not take him on as a legal client, since I would worry about getting stiffed."

"Doña Amada also said he cheats on Doña Elsa."

"I wouldn't know about that, but he does have a reputation for flirting with women and that sometimes it gets pretty creepy and awkward."

"Amalfi said he hit on her and grabbed her rear end a few years ago."

"Gross," Benny said, sounding disgusted.

"That's exactly what I said when she told me that story.

"I wonder why Doña Elsa puts up with that shoddy behavior?" Dana asked, knowing there would be no answer forthcoming, since only Doña Elsa could answer that, and maybe even she didn't have an answer as to why she didn't send her lout of a husband packing.

"Who knows? But it's not really any of our business," Benny said.

"I know, I know, just curious is all."

"Well, you can ask her when we go up there and you meet her," Benny said facetiously.

She blushed. "I'm not touching that subject with a thousand-foot pole, and point taken, mister," Dana said, smiling. "Can you pass the crackers, please?" Dana said, getting up to scoop up some more of that delicious ceviche onto her plate.

## CHAPTER FOUR

THE NEXT MORNING, DANA SENT A TEXT MESSAGE TO MAX Perry taking him up on his offer of a private tour of the wild-flower reserve.

She felt awkward since she was cashing in on his offer so soon.

She wasn't sure if he would actually come through, since people say and offer all sorts of things when you're face-to-face then they ghost you when it comes time to make good on the offer.

Max replied right away.

"Sounds good. I'm free this afternoon. Works for you?"

Dana texted back that the afternoon would be awesome and she thanked him for making it happen.

They exchanged a couple more texts, agreeing to meet at the front entrance of the reserve at two o'clock p.m.

Dana was excited about the upcoming visit, but Ramón seemed even more excited when she told him that she was going up there.

Ramón Villalobos was Dana's caretaker, and he was an

amazing gardener with the greenest thumb and landscaping skills she had ever seen.

When she told him about her upcoming visit to the reserve, he began to tell her about the orchids there and how Doña Elsa's orchids were breathlessly beautiful. A real source of natural beauty and the most amazing orchid collection in the province. "Make sure she shows them to you, because they're off the beaten path deep in the reserve."

"The way you describe them, they'll have to drag me out of the reserve kicking and screaming if I don't get to see those orchids," Dana reassured him with a smile.

DANA ARRIVED at Benny's beach house at one o'clock p.m. He had offered to pick her up, but she declined, insisting on driving them herself. The reserve was up in the mountains, and Dana loved driving her 1948 Jeep Willys—which she had nick-named "Big Red" for its cherry red paint job. It was especially fun driving Big Red in the wild with the soft top off, so she told Benny she would pick him up.

He got into the passenger seat, buckled in, and teasingly gave the sign of the cross.

She laughed. She knew her lead-footed reputation and driving like she was trying to evade a police dragnet was well deserved. Her best friend Courtney swore the only thing scarier than Captain Junior's puddle jumper airplane ride from San José to Mariposa Beach was being a passenger with Dana behind the wheel of Big Red.

It was a beautiful sunny day, so she had the soft top of Big Red rolled down so they could enjoy the feeling of the warm tropical breeze infused with the fragrant smells of the forest. She could smell the sea salt in the air as it came wafting over from the Pacific Ocean. Even though they had to put up with a mouthful or two of dust from the mostly gravel roads from Mariposa Beach towards the reserve, it was worth it.

The reserve was about a thirty-minute drive from Mariposa Beach. Most of it was straight up the mountainside, which reminded Dana of driving on Divisadero Street in San Francisco with its steep incline from the NoPa neighborhood up towards Pacific Heights before it plunged down like a rollercoaster ride into the Marina District.

But unlike San Francisco, the traffic around Mariposa Beach was almost nonexistent. She passed a few campesinos—farmers. One campesino was cutting foliage on the side of the road with his trusty machete. The second campesino they drove past was herding cattle right by the road. She gave them a friendly honk as she maneuvered Big Red around his herd. The old man with a leathery face and gray mustache waved. He had a big smile on his face despite the fact he was missing most of his front teeth. A look of surprise crossed his face, no doubt from seeing the pretty gringa driving by in the little red Jeep.

Even a few of the cows turned their heads to look at Dana and Benny with indifference as they lazily chewed cud and swatted flies away with their tails.

Dana beamed.

"You really like driving out here, don't you?" Benny asked, watching her.

"It's a blast. What's not to like?" Dana replied, pressing down on the accelerator, forcing Benny to hold on to the side grip bar handle.

"Spending time with an expat new to the country is a great way to make me appreciate the beauty we have here in Costa Rica. It's easy to forget about it and take it for granted, especially in the city where my blood pressure goes up a few notches every time I'm behind the wheel," Benny said wistfully.

"I can relate. I lived in one of the most beautiful cities in the world. Golden Gate Park, the bridge, the Marin Headlands, the redwoods, but you forget about all that when you're in the mix of the chaos of the city or stuck on Muni wondering why the train car hasn't moved in five minutes."

They continued on their way with Benny giving Dana directions to the reserve. She took a hard right a bit too fast as Big Red skidded a bit on gravel.

"Good Lordy, you know I'm giving you directions far in advance with the hopes that you slow down before making those sharp wide turns on these dirt roads. I feel like I'm going to fly right off the side. And it's a long drop down the mountain, you know."

Dana laughed.

"Seriously, take a look down the mountainside. You might see a car or two down there from others who took a curve a wee bit too fast," Benny said, glancing down into the steep precipice.

"They don't remove the cars?"

"Not always. Or at least not in the old days. It was too risky. So they removed the bodies, since I doubt anyone could survive that fall, but left the vehicles down there, serving like a macabre PSA to slow down and not take those curves as fast as you're taking them," Benny said, adding a loud "ahem" right after in case she didn't catch the hint. She did. Then she chuckled and pressed on the accelerator again.

"Dana!" Benny pleaded, turning white.

They arrived at the Reserve at 1:40. Dana parked and looked at her watch. "Hmm, we're early."

"Not too surprising, Dale Earnhardt," Benny said as the color began to return to his ashen face.

They exited the vehicle as two blonde young girls approached. They looked like Nordic beauty queens.

Benny must have seen the confusion in her face seeing the

Viking goddesses in the tropics, because he leaned in and said, "Interns from the foreign exchange program."

The two women walked up to them and introduced themselves. Iris Kjellberg was from Sweden and Lydia Bock was from Germany. Both were bioengineering undergraduate students.

"Are there a lot of foreign exchange students here?" Dana asked.

Iris and Lydia looked at each other as they thought it over. "About fifteen or twenty," Lydia said as Iris nodded in agreement.

"Wow, big program," Dana said.

"It's a big reserve. An incredible learning opportunity," Lydia said.

"There are flowers here that can't be easily found out on the wild," Iris added.

"Especially for students like us from Europe, we don't get a lot of opportunities to study tropical flora," Lydia said.

"It sounds like a wonderful program. We're here to meet with Max Perry, do you know him?"

Both students lit up like a Christmas tree. Dana figured the good-looking scientist would have that effect on most women, especially a pair of twenty-year-old college girls.

Dana saw Benny smiling awkwardly. He was accustomed to women having similar reactions about him, but he was like yesterday's news, especially when he told the students he was a lawyer and the smiles turned into frowns as if he had told them he clubbed baby seals for a living.

"Oh, yes, he's a brilliant biologist," Lydia said, replying to Dana.

"He's in charge of the plant biology students for this semester. You can find him up in the main building. Unless he's out in the field, he should be there," Iris said, pointing at a building up the road behind them.

"He's expecting us, so he should be there," Dana said. They thanked the students and made their way towards the building.

"Looks like those girls have a crush on Max," Dana said, giggling as they walked.

"Seems that way," Benny said.

They were just about to reach the building when they heard a blood-curdling scream from inside which sent shivers up and down their spines.

# CHAPTER FIVE

THE SCREAMS COMING FROM INSIDE THE MAIN BUILDING of the reserve made Dana's toes curl, and her first instinct was to run in the opposite direction of the screaming.

Her mind went to the thought that there was an active shooter inside unleashing carnage or some other horrible scenarios that made her want to run back to Big Red and speed back towards Mariposa Beach.

All these thoughts whirled around her head for mere seconds when she heard Benny say, "Someone needs help," and he ran towards the building.

Dana thought about it for another second and decided to run after Benny to see what was going on. Perhaps she could be of help as well.

The screams had come from a young woman in her early twenties. She was distraught and in tears as she came out running from the building so fast that she almost stumbled down the front steps.

Lucky for her, a young man popped out of the crowd of curious onlookers that had formed at the bottom of the front steps of the building to catch her before she tumbled to the ground. She buried her face into the young man's chest sobbing as he tried to comfort her.

They were soon joined by an older man in his forties who was dressed in landscaping work clothes. He also tried to calm her down as he asked her questions.

"What happened?"

"Are you hurt?"

The young man continued to hold her, telling her to breathe and reassuring her that everything was going to be all right.

An even bigger crowd had gathered around the distraught woman. Mostly young students part of the exchange program.

Dana heard someone call the distraught woman Alice.

Iris and Lydia had joined the collection of befuddled onlookers.

"What happened?" Lydia asked Dana and Benny as she sidled up next to them.

"I have no idea. We were just about to go inside when we heard terrible screaming and she came running outside. She's too freaked out to speak clearly," Dana replied.

"It must be something really bad. I've never seen Alice get fazed by anything," Lydia said, sounding scared.

"Is she a student too?" Dana asked.

"Yes, Alice Mora, she's from Texas," Iris replied.

"You don't mess with Texas," Lydia said in almost a trance like whisper.

Dana looked at Lydia, confused.

"Alice said that all the time," Iris explained.

At that moment Dana saw Max Perry and an older woman running from the back of the building towards the crowd.

"That's Max," Dana whispered to Benny.

"That's Doña Elsa with him," Benny whispered back.

The older man that was attending to Alice was dressed in a khaki shirt and shorts. He wore a wide brim Panama Jack hat.

He kept trying to figure out what had freaked Alice out so badly as the young man continued holding her tightly in his arms, trying to calm her down.

"Who's the man in the hat talking to Alice?" Dana asked the girls.

Iris replied, "That's Claro Madderra, Doña Elsa's right-hand man. He manages the day-to-day of the reserve. The young guy is a fellow student, Chris from Michigan."

Claro Madderra was tall, with a dark complexion a mixture of his genes and a lifetime working outdoors in the tropics. He wore a thick droopy horseshoe mustache that was as black as the color of his hair.

Chris was slender with moppy brown hair it was quite the contrast seeing both men side-by-side.

Doña Elsa joined them. She faced the distraught Alice and she gently took Alice's hands into hers and held them.

"Someone get her a glass of water," Doña Elsa said.

One of the students ran off and came back quickly with the glass of water which he nervously gave to Doña Elsa. She in turn handed it to Alice who's hands were trembling.

"Drink some water, honey,' Doña Elsa said.

Dana was in awe how tiny Doña Elsa seemed next to Claro. As a matter of fact, it seemed that everyone towered over her. Dana was struck by how diminutive she was. Her hair was brown with natural grey streaks. She wore it long down and was dressed in similar khaki attire as Claro Madderra and Max Perry.

She was stocky but not overweight. Even though she was petite, she commanded an aura of leadership, which was made evident as soon as she walked up to the crowd and began to take control over the situation.

Max Perry saw Dana standing there and he nodded her way to acknowledge that he had seen her, but he didn't walk over towards her, staying next to Doña Elsa's side as they tried to figure out what had happened to Alice.

It was Doña Elsa who finally got Alice to calm down enough to convey what had happened to her that sent her on the edge of a nervous breakdown.

One of the dozen or so students that had gathered around handed Alice a glass of water which trembled in her hand, spilling water as she brought it to her lips and drank from the glass.

"Honey, what is wrong?" Doña Elsa asked, sounding like a concerned grandmother.

"I can't... not to you ... I can't say," she said between sobs and sips of water.

"You can tell me anything, sweetheart. Please, you're scaring everyone here," Doña Elsa said.

"It's Don Eladio. He's... he's... he's dead. It's horrible, horrible," Alice managed to say before breaking down in sobs once again, dropping the glass to the ground as she buried her quivering face into her hands. Her knees buckled as Claro steadied her to prevent her from collapsing to the ground.

Dana looked at Benny. "Eladio. As in Doña Elsa's husband," she whispered. He shrugged his shoulders in disbelief.

Everyone looked shell-shocked.

Doña Elsa remained calm and collected, which surprised Dana, since she had just been told her husband was dead.

"You must be mistaken, honey. Where did you see him?"

Alice took a deep breath. "Inside. By the greenhouse in the main building. I'm sorry, Doña Elsa, but... but... he's dead, and it's horrible."

"Are you sure he's dead? Maybe he needs help," Chris said.

Alice looked at him, her lips quivering, and said, "He had a hedge shear in his chest." She went back into Chris's arms, shaking like a leaf.

"It's horrible," she said once again as she began to sob uncontrollably.

"Go to the dorm room and have her lie down," Doña Elsa told Chris. Then she turned to Max Perry and said, "Call the police." Then she turned to Claro Madderra. "Help me find him to see what's going on."

Madderra nodded. "Of course."

Doña Elsa turned to the gathered crowd. "Everyone else, please stay here in the courtyard until we figure out what's going on."

Having said that, she turned to Claro and said, "Let's go." They went up the front steps into the building.

Everyone stood there dumbfounded, Dana and Benny included. She couldn't believe what they were seeing and hearing.

"Good grief, you think she's right, he's dead?"

Benny shrugged. "I don't know, but the way that girl is acting, I believe at the very least Eladio is hurt badly in there."

"I hope you're right and that he's just hurt and not really dead."

But all Dana could envision was a man lying there with hedge shears sticking out of his chest.

She shivered. Benny put his arms around her.

"What should we do?"

"Nothing we can do right now. I would imagine the police will want to talk to everyone that's here, so we better stick around and wait," Benny said.

Even though it was another hot day in the tropics, Dana shivered again. She looked around and noticed everyone had a worried look on their face. And they were way up in the mountain in the middle of nowhere. It would be a while before the cavalry would arrive.

Dana and Benny were there for about twenty minutes.

They talked mostly with Iris and Lydia until Chris showed up. He had been the fellow student that had been trying to calm Alice down.

He gave Lydia a half-wave as he made his way towards them.

"How's Alice?" Lydia asked as Chris joined the group.

"Not good. She's really freaked out," Chris said.

"I don't blame her, I don't know how I would react if I ever found a dead body," Lydia said.

Dana and Benny gave each other a furtive glance. Unfortunately for Dana, she knew exactly what it felt like to find a dead body. It was a shock to the system that haunts your dreams long after. But she wasn't about to share that tidbit of information with these kids.

"Especially someone that was murdered," Chris said.

"How do you know he was murdered?" Dana asked.

Chris gave her a *who are you* look.

Lydia introduced them.

"This is Benny and Dana. They live in Mariposa Beach. She's the owner of Books, Bagels, and Lattes."

"Well, I own the bookstore part, and my friend Mindy owns the bagels and lattes part," Dana corrected.

Chris shook Benny's and Dana's hands.

"I'm Chris Turner. I'm a student at Northwestern doing an internship at the reserve."

"Why did Alice think he was murdered?" Dana asked him again.

"She didn't say that, but she said Don Eladio had a hedge shear sticking out of his chest; I doubt that could have been an accident," Chris explained.

"So what's next for you guys?" Dana asked.

Chris looked at Lydia and they shrugged their shoulders in unison.

"I don't know what's going to happen with the reserve but Doña Elsa *is* the reserve," Chris said, sounding despondent. "I better go check on Alice," he said as he turned back to head towards the student quarters. Lydia followed him as the rest of the crowd began to dissipate, with most of the students heading to the student quarters as well. The quarters were a concrete building that didn't look very nice to Dana. It reminded her of the public restroom buildings at the national parks. Grey cinder block built for its utilitarian purpose of housing many students with no frills.

"What now?" Dana asked Benny. But before he could answer, Max Perry came out from the main building and he walked up towards Dana and Benny.

"So sorry you had to be here for all that," Max said.

"Don't worry about that," Dana said.

Dana realized with all the commotion she hadn't introduced Benny to Max, so she did so.

The two men shook hands and exchanged a quick awkward greeting.

"Sorry we have to meet under these circumstances," Max said.

"Did you find out if he's really dead?" Benny asked about Don Eladio.

"Claro just confirmed it before I came out here. He's dead."

"Oh jeez," Dana said.

"How's Doña Elsa holding up?" Benny asked.

"Doña Elsa is one tough cookie. Right now she wants to make sure the kids are going to be okay and that this won't affect the reserve," Max said.

Dana thought that was puzzling, being that her husband was dead and apparently a victim of a violent attack.

"Chris said Alice is certain that Don Eladio was murdered, is that true?" Dana asked.

Max shrugged his shoulders and said, "I don't know. But Claro confirmed that a pair of garden shears did the job. Doesn't look like that it was an accident."

"Oh, my," Dana said. "Is the body still inside?"

"Yes. We didn't move it. Claro is standing guard by the body. The students are rallying around Doña Elsa to comfort her and to protect her just in case there is a killer on the loose in the reserve."

That statement caused Dana to visibly shake. Could one of those students be the killer?

# CHAPTER SIX

DANA AND BENNY DECIDED THAT IT DIDN'T HAVE TO WAIT around. The whole ordeal gave them the creeps and it would take awhile for the police to get to the remote location so they headed back to Casa Verde.

Unlike the fun ride up to the reserve, the ride back to Casa Verde was a somber one.

Benny and Dana didn't talk much.

Alice Mora's screams kept playing on a loop in Dana's head.

She tried to shut them off but they just kept on playing over and over in her head.

Dana drove Big Red back to Casa Verde. She clicked on the remote control to open her front gate.

"I don't want to be the one to tell Ramón about what just went down at the reserve," Dana said as she waited for the gate to open.

Once open, she drove through the open front gate and onto her long driveway and parked. Right away she saw Ramón walking to the car excitedly.

"Oh, man, here we go," Dana said.

"It's okay, he'll want to know what's going on so he can check on Doña Elsa."

Dana climbed out of Big Red.

"Aren't those the most beautiful orchids you've ever seen?" Ramón asked her, sounding excited.

Dana and Benny exchanged a nervous glance. Ramón was close to Doña Elsa. Like most of the working poor in the district, they all knew and loved Doña Elsa. A young Ramón had developed his love of orchids and gardening from Doña Elsa and credited her with his landscaping skills.

"Unfortunately, we weren't able to see them or get the tour," Dana replied sheepishly.

Ramón looked so disappointed, but his facial expression quickly turned to concern, sensing something bad happened.

"Is everything okay with Doña Elsa?" he asked.

"She's okay physically, but her husband is dead," Benny said.

Dana sighed. She felt relieved it was Benny who told him.

"What? How?" Ramón asked.

"Well, we don't know for sure yet, but it appears he might have been murdered," Dana said, looking down at the ground.

Ramón peppered Dana and Benny with questions, but they didn't have any answers.

His wife, Carmen, joined them. She, too, was shocked when Ramón told her that Don Eladio was dead.

"I can't believe it," Carmen said, giving herself the sign of the cross.

"I feel terrible. I didn't like Don Eladio because he treated Doña Elsa badly, but I can't believe someone would kill him. And poor Doña Elsa. No matter what, they had been married for forty years."

"Did they have any children?" Dana asked.

"Yes, a son and a daughter. Both grown. Living in San José," Ramón said.

"Why didn't you like Don Eladio?" Dana asked.

Ramón's mouth tightened.

"I don't mean to talk bad about the dead, but..." Ramón was hesitant.

"He was not good to Doña Elsa," Carmen spoke for him.

Ramón nodded in agreement.

"I've yet to hear anyone have a good word about him," Dana said.

"He was very friendly and charming, hard not to like him when he was putting on the charm. Like a used-car salesman," Benny said.

"He was very disrespectful to Doña Elsa. He was always cheating on her with many women, including some of the interns," Ramón said, sounding disgusted.

"Oh, gross, those students are in their early twenties," Dana said.

"Exactly," Ramón said. "And he doesn't help at all financially. He hasn't even worked in twenty years. Sits around coming with get-rich-quick schemes while living off her hard work, and he didn't even appreciate her hard work," Ramón said.

"He was always up to no good with his business ideas, which would end up putting the reserve in financial troubles," Carmen said.

"Doña Elsa lost the support of one of the schools a couple years ago. Don Eladio kept hitting on the female students, so the school pulled its funding of the reserve and stopped sending students over. It cost the reserve a lot of money, resources, and it hurt the reserve's reputation. Doña Elsa was furious," Ramón added.

"I hadn't thought about that," Dana said. "I would imagine

the schools and parents of these students are going to freak out when they learn there was a murder on the reserve."

"I would have my daughter on the first plane out," Benny added.

"I'm going to try to call Doña Elsa. See if there is anything I can do for her," Ramón said, pulling out his mobile phone from his pocket and walking away hurriedly, heading towards his house.

"I would imagine she's going to be hard to get a hold of, since she's going to be tied up with the police," Benny called after Ramón.

"I'll leave a message then, letting her know I'm thinking about her," Ramón said as he kept on walking.

"He's very upset. They were very close, like mother and son," Carmen said to Dana and Benny. Then she took off after her husband.

"Poor guy," Dana said.

"Yeah, he must feel helpless, which is one of the worst feelings to have when someone you care for is going through something terrible," Benny said. They stood out by the carport as Ramón and Carmen walked out of sight.

Ramón and Carmen's home was located about two hundred feet from Casa Verde. It had been a strange arrangement for Dana when she first inherited the property, but now she couldn't imagine what it would be like to live on the property without Ramón and Carmen nearby.

It broke her heart to see how distraught Ramón appeared to be over all this, but she would give him his space as he tried to get his mind around what was happening to the beloved Doña Elsa.

Dana and Benny went inside the house.

"Boy, I need a drink," Dana said.

"Me too," Benny said in agreement.

She went into the kitchen and took out two bottles of Imperial beer. They sipped on the beer while sitting on counter stools around the kitchen island.

"Do you think the police are going to want to talk to us?" Dana asked.

Benny shrugged his shoulders. "Well... since we were there when he died, I would imagine that the police will want to take statements from anyone who was there when the murder happened."

Dana shivered. It seemed whenever there was a murder near Mariposa Beach, she was around—an observation that the lead homicide investigator in the district for the Costa Rican Judicial Police had previously shared with her. *And now here we go again*, Dana thought as she sighed heavily.

# CHAPTER SEVEN

Bagels, Books, and Lattes was abuzz, and it wasn't just from the caffeine being served up by Mindy. Word about Don Eladio's death had made its way from the reserve all the way down the mountain and to the tiny beach town of Mariposa Beach like an out-of-control wildfire.

Everyone was talking about it, but the jabber charge was led, as usual, by the town's Gossip Brigade, a quartet of old biddies who seemed to dig up the town dirt with the efficiency of a backhoe.

As soon as the Gossip Brigade were at the cafe, Leo Salas poked his head out of the kitchen. "What's the word around the campfire, ladies?" he asked the Brigade with a smile.

"Don't encourage them," Mindy muttered back at him under her breath.

It was too late. Doña Amada smiled wide and breathed in deeply to pass along the latest news like a town crier.

"Looks like good old Elsa finally had enough of that lout, so she did some necessary trimming with her trusty hedge shears," said Doña Amada with a smirk.

She was the octogenarian leader of the Brigade who didn't

seem to have a filter between the thoughts that popped in her head and the words that went out of her mouth.

Dana was certain that if you looked up the meaning of "suffers no fools," you would find a picture of Doña Amada in the description.

"Oh, you're awful, Amada," said Doña Chilla. At seventy-eight, she was the youngest member of the Brigade, and as far as Dana was concerned, she was the nicest one of the group. A sweet old lady that tried, in vain, to keep Doña Amada from going too far off the rails with her ranting.

"Really?" Leo said. "The police arrested her or something?"

"Not yet," Doña Amada replied, putting the emphasis on "yet" as if to imply an arrest was imminent.

Dana was over on the bookstore side of the cafe, eavesdropping. "I wonder if there is any truth to that," she spoke softly to Amalfi, who shrugged her shoulders.

"Seems to me they get a lot of their facts wrong," she replied after a moment.

Dana laughed. "You're absolutely right."

Dana chided herself for putting too much stock into what the Gossip Brigade said, but it still didn't stop her from wondering if there was any validity to what Doña Amada was saying.

"I guess only time will tell," she said.

"Who told you that hogwash?" a voice boomed from the front door of the cafe.

Dana and the others hadn't seen him entering the cafe just as the Gossip Bride began their gossip, and were caught off guard. Dana was mortified with embarrassment.

The gossipy chatter died down as everyone looked over at Max Perry, who stood there with a look of disdain on his face and his arms crossed in front of his chest.

"That's what I heard, and it really shouldn't come as too

much of a surprise. Eladio has treated her with little respect since they were newlyweds. You wouldn't know, since you're an outsider and have only been here for a few weeks. I've been for a few decades, sonny," Doña Amada said in a huff.

"A few decades? I think eight plus decades is more than a few," said Doña Luz, the comedian of the Brigade, lightening the mood as people started laughing and Doña Amada blushed.

Dana herself couldn't help but chuckle, but she quickly regained her composure. There had been a lot of speculation and gossip that she had murdered her cousin, who had contested her inheritance, when she first moved to Mariposa Beach, so she knew it wasn't any fun to be gossiped about. She tried to avoid going down that rabbit hole of town gossip.

"I'm just saying, let's leave the speculation to the police as they do their job," Perry said. He walked up to the counter and ordered a dark roast coffee and a sesame bagel with jalapeño cream cheese from Mindy.

The Gossip Bridge shuffled on out as they headed over to their reserved table at the Qué Vista restaurant, where they played canasta twice a week in the midafternoon.

"Good luck with your game, ladies," Leo said as they left without saying anything else.

Perry walked over to Dana while he waited for his bagel.

"How are you holding up?" Dana asked him.

"Sorry, I shouldn't have butted in, but I hate gossip," he said. He seemed embarrassed about getting into it with Doña Amada.

"Well, it's the lifeline of a small town. You need to get used to it or it will drive you bonkers," Dana said.

"I suppose," he said, not sounding convinced.

"So there isn't any truth about what Doña Amada said?" Dana asked.

"The police are talking to everyone, but it's not like they've arrested Doña Elsa or anything like that," he said.

"Is Detective Picado leading the investigation?"

"He is, you know him?"

Dana smiled. "Unfortunately, I do."

Perry looked at her, puzzled.

"Lets just say we're not exchanging Christmas cards."

"He does seem to be a bit rough around the edges," Perry said.

"That's a polite way of putting it," Dana said.

"He wanted a list of everyone who was there when Don Eladio died, so sorry, hate to get you involved in this, but I had to give him your and Benny's names," Perry said, seeming embarrassed.

"It's okay, Benny and I figured as much. Not like there is anything we have to contribute," Dana said.

"So you didn't see anything or anyone acting suspicious?"

"No. We had just arrived. We were chatting with a couple students who were showing us where to find you when all Cain broke loose. How about you? See anything suspicious?"

Perry seemed taken aback by the question.

"Me? No, not all."

"But you were inside when it happened?"

"I was in the office doing paperwork, waiting for you guys. Don Eladio was in the southwest arboretum, where he was killed. So I didn't see anything suspicious until I heard Alice's screams like everyone else."

"That poor girl, how is she doing?"

"She's doing better. The mass exodus of students has already begun, and Alice is desperate to go back home to Texas, but the police won't let her leave just yet since she's their prime witness. Her parents are flying in tonight, though, so that should be of some comfort for the poor thing," Perry said.

Just then Mindy called for Perry; his order was ready.

He said goodbye to Dana and picked up his bagel and coffee and walked outside.

Dana looked out the window and she saw that loudmouth from the other day approach Perry. The two seemed to have a heated conversation as Perry stormed off. The loudmouth walking behind him was saying something to him, but Perry didn't turn around and didn't seem to acknowledge him any longer. He just continued walking at a brisk pace.

Dana continued to watch them until both men were out of her line of sight.

*What an odd exchange between those two,* she thought.

# CHAPTER EIGHT

DANA WAS AT HOME UNWINDING AFTER A LONG DAY AT THE bookstore slash cafe. It was almost seven p.m. Benny was going to stop by on his way back to San José. It was the part of their relationship she did not like. It was the drag of a long-distance relationship.

Benny's law practice was in the San José suburb of Escazú. His nine-year-old daughter also lived there, so he spent most of his time there.

He preferred to leave back to the city at night, since traffic was lighter during that time. The distance was about one hundred and fifty miles, but most of the freeway is a narrow two-lane road through the mountain that took over four hours on a good travel day.

Dana was in a trance when her phone rang, startling her back to reality. *Time to stop feeling sorry for yourself,* she thought as she picked up her mobile phone.

It was Detective Gabriela Rojas. *Oh, brother,* Dana thought as she took the call.

"Hey, what's up?" she said.

"Hi Dana, hope things are going well for you," Rojas replied.

Dana and the detective had become friends. She couldn't say the same about Rojas's partner, Detective Juan Picado. *Rough around the edges*, she remembered how Max Perry had described him earlier in that day. *More like rough all over, inside and out*, she thought.

After meandering chitchat for about a minute, Rojas got to the crux of the matter.

"Your name came up as a possible witness to the murder of Eladio Calderón."

"Oh my gosh, so he was murdered," Dana said.

"His death has been officially ruled a homicide," Rojas confirmed. "Did you see anything suspicious or anyone that didn't seem to belong there?"

"Not at all. It was my first time there, so not sure who wouldn't belong there, but all I saw were students and staff. Nothing seemed out of line to me."

"And what were you doing there?"

"I met Max Perry, who is doing research there, at my bookstore, and he told me about the reserve. I mentioned I'd been meaning to visit but hadn't made it up there yet, so he offered me a personalized tour. Seemed too good to pass up, so Benny and I headed up there the next day."

"I see. Did you get the tour? Was Max Perry with you when Don Eladio was murdered?"

"Well, no, we had just arrived. We were making our way to the building to look for Max when we heard that young girl, Alice, screaming, and she came running out of the building looking petrified."

"Did you see Mr. Perry at all?"

"Yes, after all the commotion, he came out to see what was going on."

"He came out of where?" Rojas asked.

"From the main building where the offices are located."

"How did he look to you?"

"I don't know, he seemed concerned for Alice, who was crying. By the way, how is she doing?"

"She's doing fine. Shook up is all. So, Dana, about Max? How was he acting?"

"Acting?"

"Yes, was he acting suspicious or strange?"

That question made Dana shudder. "Do you think he had anything—"

Rojas cut her off. "We don't know anything yet, I'm just covering all the bases for everyone who was there."

"Okay. No, he wasn't acting suspicious or strange, he just seemed worried about Alice."

"Is Benny there?"

"Not yet. He said he was going to stop on his way up to San José."

"Okay, I better call him before he's out of town," Rojas said.

Dana wanted to ask Rojas a million questions, but all she blurted out was to ask about Detective Picado's reaction when her name came up.

"About what you expect," Rojas said. It sounded like she was holding back a chuckle.

"I can imagine, another murder investigation and my name comes up, again," Dana said. It was funny in a morbid sort of way, but it made Dana sad.

"Am I some sort of bad luck magnet or something?"

"I don't know, but I'm going to start wearing a clove of garlic around my neck around you," Rojas said, laughing.

"Hardy har-har," was Dana's response.

"I have to go, but listen, think about that day. Think hard. Dig deep down in your subconscious. Maybe there was a strange car or person that you didn't put too much stock into them but now in hindsight maybe it's something we should check out."

"Okay. Is Doña Elsa a suspect?"

"Come on, Dana, I couldn't tell you one way or another right now. So think about that day. I have to go," Rojas said, hanging up the phone.

DANA SAT ON HER SOFA. She had been reading Stephen King's creepy *The Outsider* before the call, but now she was feeling even more creeped out with what was going on in real life to continue reading it. She turned off her Kindle and put it down on the sofa. Her cat, Wally, jumped on the sofa and lay on the Kindle.

"You're weird," Dana said, petting the cat that purred. "I guess you like it because it's a little warm."

She started to think back to the last couple days as she petted Wally.

*Is there anything I overlooked?*

Then she thought about the loudmouth. It struck her that she kept seeing him turning up whenever Max Perry was around. And the two men exchanged words at the bookstore for the way the loudmouth was berating Mindy for having run out of the cream cheese he wanted. Then he seemed to be lurking around the reserve on that day. And then she saw him and Max appear to be in another heated conversation outside of the bookstore slash cafe earlier that day.

Her phone buzzed the announcement of an incoming text message. The house had been quiet as a mouse, and she was so lost in thought that the sudden sound of the incoming text made her jump out of her skin, freaking out Wally, who jumped off and ran away.

"Some protector you are," she said as she looked at her phone. It was a text from Benny letting her know he was pulling up in his Land Cruiser. She had given him his own remote control doohickey so he didn't have to ring the intercom buzzard out front, but he always sent her a text message warning so he wouldn't freak her out. She laughed, thinking how the text message sound had done just that—freaked her out... big time.

She blamed it on the weird aura abound due to the murder, her conversation with Detective Rojas, and most of all, Stephen King.

"What's wrong?" Benny asked when he saw her.

She could see the worry in his face, especially in his brown eyes.

"I look that bad?" she teased.

"No, you looked spooked."

She smiled. They were getting to know each other so well.

"Oh, it's just everything that's going on with the murder, and I was reading a really scary book by Stephen King and I got myself all freaked out."

He joined her on the couch.

"Do you want anything to drink?"

"No, thanks, I'm good. I have my big coffee mug filled to the brim for the drive back to Escazú," Benny said, smiling.

"I worry about you driving up there at night on that treacherous road."

Dana had a right to be worried. It was a winding road through the mountain with steep drop-offs with only a thin-looking guardrail offering any sort of protection, and that was in just some spots. For large stretches of road there was nothing to stop a car from driving off the road and down a steep hillside into a forested oblivion.

The trip includes driving through the highest point of the Inter-American Highway in Costa Rica at an elevation of over 11,000 feet, known as the Cerro de la Muerte—Hill of Death—since many travelers have succumbed to it, plummeting to their death down below. Car wreckages are still visible down below, since it was deemed too dangerous to recover the wrecked vehicles.

Toss in the crazy driving that goes on the roads in Costa Rica, and it's a drive not for the faint of heart, especially at night.

"I've been driving back and forth between Escazú and Mariposa Beach since I was a kid. I could probably do it blindfolded," Benny said.

He then changed the subject. "So Detective Rojas called you."

"Nice subject change, mister. Yes, she called me. I take it she called you as well?"

"On my way over here."

"Did you have any useful information to give her?"

"No. You?"

"Nope. But you know, I started to think..."

"Uh-oh."

"Shush, you! Anyway, as I was saying, I started to think about the day leading up to our drive up to the reserve, and remember that rude customer I told you about?"

"The one that was nasty to Mindy over cream cheese and was critical about your book inventory?"

"Yes, him. Well, he seemed a bit unhinged."

"That's a big stretch from being an annoying and demanding customer at the cafe to being a killer."

"I didn't say he was a killer, just that he seemed unhinged. Anger-management issues."

Dana went on to explain the heated exchanges she had seen him have with Max Perry.

"Do you think I should let Gabriela know about him?" Dana asked.

Benny seemed to mull it over for a moment.

"Well, I hate jamming anyone up with the police unnecessarily, but the fact you're thinking about him in that way, it can't hurt to call her. She's the law enforcement professional, and she'll be able to determine if there is anything to it. Might as well err on the side of caution versus letting a killer roam freely to possibly harm someone else," Benny said.

Dana called Detective Rojas but got her voicemail, so she left her a message.

"You've done your part," Benny said as he got up from the couch. "I better get going so I don't get home too late." They embraced and kissed.

AFTER BENNY LEFT, Dana made her way upstairs to her bedroom. It was eight p.m. Too early for bed. She looked at her Kindle but couldn't take any more of Mr. King, being all alone in that quiet house. Especially since sooner rather than later the howler monkeys that lived out in the trees on the other side of her property's wall would start barking at the moon.

She turned on the TV and fired up Netflix and scrolled for what seemed like an hour, looking for something lighthearted to watch. She settled on *Dirty Dancing*. Sure, she'd seen that movie about twenty times, but it was one of her favorite movies, and she wanted to watch something she enjoyed to easer her into sleep. She hit play. *Nobody puts Baby in the corner*, she thought as the movie started.

## CHAPTER NINE

Dana woke up at seven in the morning. *Dirty Dancing* had been just what the doctor ordered. She fell asleep before Johnny Castle triumphantly hoisted Baby up in the air as Bill Medley and Jennifer Warnes belted out about having the time of their lives.

She went out on a quick run on the beach. It was muggy out there already, so she came back feeling extra moist. She made herself some oatmeal with a banana picked from a tree in her backyard. She brewed some coffee and drank it while reading the *Tico Times* online to see what was going on in the expat community. She showered and was on her way to the bookstore slash cafe by eight forty-five.

Mindy and Leo arrived to open the cafe part of the bookstore at six thirty am, since the morning rush started as soon as they opened for business at seven. The bookstore side of the business didn't open until nine a.m..

She was parking Big Red when her phone rang. It was Detective Rojas.

Dana answered, "Hey, how are you?"

"Good. Sorry I didn't reply to your voicemail, but things got very hectic after we spoke," Rojas said.

Dana's curiosity was piqued.

"Oh, what happened?" Dana asked, trying not to sound too eager.

"Well, let's just say your loudmouth guy is a moot point. We arrested Doña Elsa at the reserve late last night."

Dana was stunned. She almost dropped the phone. She didn't even know her, but everyone spoke so fondly about her that she felt like she was a friend and that there was no way she could have killed her husband, no matter how badly he had treated her over the years. And that was one of the first things that popped in her head. It seemed everyone and their brother and sister knew he was a no-good lout. Doña Elsa knew, since there had been numerous break-ups and get-back-togethers in their marriage, so why would she snap now? After all those years?

"I can't believe it." That was all Dana could say.

"I know. Trust me, I grew up in the district and know her well. I'm shocked, but the evidence doesn't lie."

"What evidence?"

"You know I can't tell you that. I shouldn't even have told you about us arresting Doña Elsa, but I know how fast word gets around in these parts, so figured I would let you know since you seemed a bit spooked about that guy. He's probably just a typical rude customer. Annoying, but harmless."

"I guess so," Dana said.

"Do me a favor, don't tell anyone I told you. Detective Picado will read me the riot act if he finds out I told you."

"Especially me of all people, right?"

"That's right," Rojas said with a chuckle. "I have to get going. Talk to you later."

Dana sat in her Jeep for about a minute after hanging up the phone. She felt terrible for Ramón. How was he going to take the news that his beloved Doña Elsa has been arrested for murder? And what about the reserve? And Max Perry and his research? And all those young students. What a crummy way to start the day.

The rest of the day was a blur. Dana did let Mindy in on the news. She was her best friend in town, and she trusted her to keep her secret. Mindy was flabbergasted to hear the news, but then the cafe got busy, so they didn't talk much about it anyway.

Dana liked it when things got busy; it made the day go by faster.

By noon, word was out. Doña Amada was, of course, the eager news breaker.

"Did you hear the news?" she cooed proudly as she walked into the cafe.

"No, what?" Mindy asked. She glanced at Dana and winked.

"I heard that Eladio, that dirty old man, got mixed up with one of the young student. You know, romantically. So I guess, Doña Elsa finally had enough of that no-good husband of her and she killed him. They arrested her for his murder. She's in jail as we speak."

She looked so proud of herself that Dana wanted to burst her little bubble and tell her that she already knew that. She had known for hours already about Doña Elsa's arrest . But she kept her mouth shut. She didn't want to get Detective Rojas in trouble, so she let the old biddy have her moment.

The part of Eladio getting involved with one of the students was news to her though. She wondered if that was true. She found that hard to believe since all the students she saw at the reserve were in their early twenties and Eladio was pushing seventy. *Gross*, she thought.

It was the talk of the cafe for the rest of the day.

Dana had been wondering how Max Perry was taking the news. Since it seemed everyone knew about the arrest, she texted him.

"Just heard about Doña Elsa. How are you doing? How are things at the reserve?"

He texted back right away.

"Wow, word travels fast. I'm fine, thanks. But the future of the reserve is bleak. I'll be in town later. We can talk then."

Dana then called Benny to give him the news.

"I'm surprised and I'm not surprised," he said.

"What the heck does that mean?" Dana said, wondering how anyone could be both surprised and not surprised.

"She's always been a feisty lady and she's put up with a lot of grief from Eladio. She must have just had enough and snapped," Benny explained.

"So what happens now?" Dana wondered. The legal system in Costa Rica was quite different than in the United States. For starters, there is no trial jury. Judges preside over a trial and they're the ones that decide if the person on trial is guilty or innocent. There is no cash bail system, so it's up to a judge to decide bail, and it's rarely granted, especially over a murder charge. So things looked bleak for Doña Elsa.

"She'll have to go through the slow wheels of the judicial system. Hopefully she can hire a good defense lawyer. If not, the state will assign one to her," Benny said.

"And the reserve?"

"She is the reserve, so unfortunately the future of the reserve looks just as bleak. Deep-pocketed developers have wanted that land for a long time, so I'm sure the legal buzzards are already starting to circle."

"How awful," Dana said, fighting back a tear. She looked up and saw Max Perry walking into the cafe.

"Oh, Max Perry is here. I'm going to see if he has any news.

I'll talk to you later," Dana said to Benny. They exchanged their goodbyes and she hung up the phone and looked up at Max Perry as he placed his order for a two-shot latte.

He then walked to the bookstore side of the cafe and up to Dana.

"Hi there," he said. He seemed a bit more chipper than she imagined.

"Hey, how are you doing with everything going on at the reserve?"

"It's going all right. I feel just terrible for Doña Elsa, but also for the reserve."

"What's going to happen to it?"

Max shrugged. "It's not looking good. The whole place is still wrapped in yellow police tape. There are only a handful of students left. As soon as the police gave the students the okay to leave the country, they left in droves. The online donations for the reserve stopped cold, and several big donors have canceled their pledges. All the affiliated universities have pulled out and told their students to leave and go back home as soon as possible. Claro has already had to start layoffs, so it will be just him, two or three student interns who work for free as volunteers, and I staying there. It's bizarre how quickly it's all fallen apart."

"Benny said Doña Elsa was the reserve, so without her it falls apart," Dana said.

"That's right. And I tried to warn her that she needed to put things in place so that wouldn't happen. She was pushing seventy after all, but she wouldn't listen and kept running things her way."

"So what are you going to do?"

"From a professional perspective, I'll be fine. I'll just finish back in Hawaii. I hate to be so cold, but I'm already lining up a new research project so I can wrap up my Ph.D.. I can't stick around here doing nothing. It's a career killer. Sorry, poor choice of words."

"It's all right. You have to do what you have to do. Nothing bad in that. What do you think is going to happen with all those flowers and orchids?"

"Claro is committed to keeping it going, so we shall see. He's a good man, but that's going to be a Herculean effort without the backing and financing of the universities and without the online donations coming in."

"And Elsa's kids, how are they doing?"

"One of them is standing behind her mother. She says there is no way she killed her father. The son is more on the outs. He didn't get along with either parent. I guess he was chomping at the bit to sell the land as his mother got older, so he might now get his wish and cash out."

"She wouldn't allow it," Dana said.

"She might not have a choice. She's land rich, cash poor. And fighting against these charges costs money. She didn't have a lot of money saved away, so she might need the cash a sale of the land would bring."

"That's so sad," Dana said.

"It sure is."

"Two-shot latte is ready," Mindy called out towards Max.

"I have to go. I need to wrap up the work I was doing before I leave."

"How much longer will you be around?" Dana asked.

"Probably not much longer. Another few days. Maybe a week," he said as he walked over towards the counter to pick up his latte. He waved back at Dana and left the cafe. He seemed to be whistling as he walked to his car.

*Boy, he's really taking things well*, Dana thought.

# CHAPTER TEN

THE NEXT DAY, DANA TOLD AMALFI SHE WOULDN'T BE IN until around eleven that morning and that she was in charge of the bookstore.

She went on another run by the beach. Showered. Had a good old tico breakfast of scrambled eggs, gallo pinto, fried ham, and a dollop of natilla. She was hungry, so she scarfed it down as if someone was going to take the plate away from her. She followed that with a small bowl of fruit: banana, pineapple, and mango. The banana and mango were plucked from the trees in her backyard. The pineapple she picked up at a roadside fruit stand near town.

She had two cups of coffee. The beans were fresh from Mindy and Leo's family coffee farm. She felt like a tica—a local—then giggled for being a silly expat who thinks she's a local.

She looked out the kitchen window that looked at her fruit trees, which Ramón tended to with such loving care and pride. She saw him out there working away, and she gulped.

He hadn't taken the news about Doña Elsa well when she told him last night.

Ramón had been chopping up yuca roots with his machete

when Dana walked up to him yesterday. They exchanged hellos and she figured she would just ask him if he had heard the news about Doña Elsa's arrest. He hadn't.

"She was arrested last night for killing her husband."

Ramón's usual smiling face and aw-shucks demeanor changed. His black eyes widened and she saw him gripping the handle of the machete harder.

"What? That can't be. She wouldn't hurt a fly," Ramón said, his voice trembling.

"Maybe it's just a mistake that will soon be rectified. The police do make mistakes in these matters," Dana said. She knew that very well. When she first moved to Mariposa Beach, the police had her pegged as a prime suspect. It was a horrible feeling to be looked in that way, people actually thinking you killed someone. And a couple months ago when a reality television star was murdered, someone else was wrongfully arrested for the crime. It worked out in the end, but it didn't change the fact that an innocent person was jailed until the justice system worked out its kinks and he was set free.

So she couldn't just assume that Doña Elsa was guilty just because she had been arrested. That's what trials are for, even though in Costa Rica there is no presumption of innocence. It's up to the defense to prove innocence to a three-judge panel.

"I know she's innocent. There is just no way," Ramón kept repeating. "What's going to happen to the reserve while she's gone?" he asked.

"I don't know, but I talked with Max Perry, a biologist who was doing research at the reserve, and he said it's not looking good for the reserve, since she was its light and shining beacon. The universities have canceled all their programs there and have called back their students and she's lost all her sponsors. So money is already drying up. Claro has had to lay off the staff," Dana said.

"This is a nightmare. Doña Elsa will be heartbroken if the reserve is closed. She's probably more worried about the future of the reserve than herself," Ramón said.

Dana thought that with Doña Elsa's freedom at stake, she would be more concerned about that than the reserve's survival, but she didn't know her. Ramón did.

"According to Max, her son is already pushing to sell the land. He claims they need money for lawyers," Dana explained.

Ramón's face hardened. "He's been trying to sell it for years. He thinks she's wasting her life tending to flowers for charity when they could sell that land for millions. He even tried to take the reserve from her, which is why they have been estranged for several years. I'm not surprised he's going to see this as an opportunity to steal her reserve so he can sell it," Ramón said, seething.

"Oh my gosh, that's horrible."

"I have to talk to Doña Elsa. At the very least I want to save those orchids. I can bring them here and take care of them here," Ramón said.

"You can do that?" Dana knew next to nothing about botany.

"Orchid transplantation is tricky, but I've done it before, so I'm confident I could save them. If a land developer gets their hands on the reserve, they'll flatten it so they can build who knows what—soulless condos, a hotel, they won't care about the rare flowers and orchids in the way."

"It will be a while before any of that happens, though."

"Yes, but if the son gets control of the reserve, he'll never allow me on the property or to take any of those orchids. I have to act now just to keep them safe."

"Do whatever you think is best. You have my full support," Dana said.

Dana finished her breakfast and cleaned up after herself.

She poured a third cup of coffee. It was eight a.m. She wanted to learn more about Doña Elsa and the reserve, which is why she didn't plan to go to the bookstore until later that morning. She went to her study instead.

It was a charming cozy nook that was surrounded by a built-in bookshelf. It was here that she had first encountered her uncle's vast collection of paperbacks as well as a valuable collection of first-edition books that almost cost her her life. It saddened her that those bad memories had spoiled the love she had for the study, since it reminded her of what had happened, but she didn't want to let those awful memories keep her away.

She sat down at her desk and began to tap away on her iMac desktop as she began Googling Doña Elsa. There were several hits of glowing articles about the work she did on behalf of Costa Rica's natural resources, as well as information from the study-abroad programs from one of the universities that sent students to the reserve. Dana figured with all the schools pulling their support, that these web pages would eventually display a 404 error page—the HTML code that a web page does not exist.

Then she saw a link to a video featuring an interview with Doña Elsa for the popular website CrazyAboutCostaRica.com. She clicked on the link and watched the video. Because of everything that went down on the day she was supposed to get her insider tour of the reserve from Max Perry, Dana didn't get a chance to meet Doña Elsa. She only saw her briefly as she tried to comfort Alice, the student that had found the body of Elsa's dead husband.

The Doña Elsa she saw on that day was in crisis mode. She didn't seem to be emotional about her husband but more about the chaos that was engulfing her reserve. The Doña Elsa from the video was relaxed, charming, and gregarious. She emitted a loving grandmotherly vibe that radiated from her body. She spoke passionately about the important work of the reserve, about protecting the nature reserve from its worst enemies: people.

She explained that by protecting nature, she created a wildlife refuge and a bioserve that attracted top scientists and students from across the globe. She was proud of her work. Dana watched her speak eloquently.

"I dream that someday one of my students or one of the researchers at my reserve might discover the cure for some of the horrible diseases that afflict mankind, right in our reserve. It's a lovely dream," she said wistfully into the camera, her eyes glistening with moisture.

Dana couldn't help but feel her eyes dampening.

She had been an investigative journalist and a reporter, so she knew people were experts at wearing masks, but Doña Elsa seemed to be speaking from the heart, and so real that it was hard to fathom she could kill anyone, let alone her husband.

The interview lasted fifteen minutes and there was something that Doña Elsa said that really made Dana think. Doña Elsa stated how she carefully partnered with universities and researchers whose mission statements aligned with hers about doing good and protecting the environment. How she was constantly turning away big money from big pharma because it was obvious that their main goal was to make gobs of money with unconscionable markups that put their products out of the hands of people that need it simply because they don't have an insurance plan that covers it if they have any at all. She was also critical of pharmaceutical companies whose focus was cosmetic vanity-type products. "They're free to pursue those goals elsewhere, but not at my reserve," she said with a steely resolve.

"You get a lot of requests from pharmaceutical companies?" the interviewer asked.

"All the time. Aggressive lot, they are. And some of them are insufferable. Especially when word got out about some of my very special orchids that can only be found at the reserve. They would love to get their hands on those orchids, but that's not going to happen as long as I'm around," Doña Elsa said with a smile and a twinkle in her eye.

That statement sent a shiver down Dana's spine.

She picked up her phone and tapped on the keys. She put the phone on speaker as it rang three times. Ramón answered the call.

"Are you still planning to go to the reserve about those orchids?" Dana asked him.

"Oh, yes. I spoke with Doña Elsa's daughter on the phone, and she's making arrangements so I can visit Doña Elsa in jail. I'm going up to the reserve to talk with Claro in an hour about it."

"Would it be okay if I tag along?"

# CHAPTER ELEVEN

Doña Elsa was being held at the OIJ offices in Nicoya. It was a substation of the Judicial Police of Costa Rica where folks arrested are held until they're transferred to the main jail to await trial or after being convicted and sentenced. Those arrested for mayor crimes—like murder—are sent to preventive imprisonment to await trail in one of the over-crowded prisons in the capital.

Benny had explained to Dana that Doña Elsa would be transferred to the Costa Rica women's prison, El Buen Pastor, that is located in the San José province in the city of San Rafael, where most women are jailed — usually for drug offenses.

Dana and Ramón drove up to the reserve to meet with Claro Madderra. Ramón spoke highly of Claro, especially for his botany skills.

Dana had seen Claro on that fateful day at the reserve, but she didn't get a chance to meet him either because of the mayhem that had been unleashed following the discovery of Don Eladio's body.

Before they left, she had texted Max Perry to let her know she was on her way to the reserve, but he hadn't replied back, which surprised her a little, since he always texted right back. She figured he was busy lining up new research work somewhere else now that the future of the reserve was in limbo and his university had pulled the plug on their partnership with the reserve, leaving him no choice but to find some other place to do his research.

DANA WAS DRIVING BIG RED. She got the feeling that Ramón wasn't too keen on being a passenger, since he had offered to drive them in his pickup several times.

They made it up to the reserve, and as soon as Dana got out of the Jeep, she noticed the startling contrast between the reserve when she was there just a few days ago.

On that day the place was a bevy of activity with students and staff everywhere; now it looked like a ghost town.

Claro Madderra greeted Ramón warmly but was a bit standoffish with Dana. She didn't blame him. He didn't know her from Adam. She was sure he was wondering why this expat was meddling and if he could trust her.

Dana's Spanish was excellent, which helped.

Dana told Claro how she was there that fateful day to meet Max Perry, who was going to give her a tour of the reserve. That seemed to put him even more at ease with her being there, but she could tell she had her work cut out if she wanted to win him over.

"How is she doing?" Ramón asked, sounding concerned.

"She's holding up. You know she's a fighter. She's tough. But I know the daylights have been scared out of her," Claro said, lowering his head.

"Are all the students gone?" Dana asked.

"There are a few holdouts left."

Dana heard a woman's voice coming from behind. She turned and saw Iris Kjellberg, the Swedish student she had met a few days ago, walking towards her. Dana smiled.

"Iris, nice to see you're still here," Dana said.

"Well, my parents aren't happy, but I wanted to stay as long as I can to see if I can be of help. I keep telling them that there is no way that Doña Elsa killed Don Eladio."

"What about Lydia?" Dana asked about the German student.

"Lydia left yesterday. Back to Hannover. She wanted to stay here, but her parents wouldn't allow it," Iris said, sounding sad.

Dana turned to Claro and asked, "So what's happening with the reserve?"

"It's shut down for now. I don't have access to the reserve's bank account to keep things going. Even if I did, her son, Mauricio, has filed an injunction freezing all the accounts, so we're in limbo."

"Is Max Perry around?"

"I haven't seen him around the last couple days. Said he's working on a new research project so he's been busy with that, but he's still staying at one of the cabanas on the reserve," Claro said.

"So what about those flowers that Ramón is worried about?"

"The wild orchids near the stream. About two miles from here. Would you like to see them?" Claro asked, sounding excited. Like he was happy to get back to talking about orchids and the reserve and not about a jailed Doña Elsa, prison, and murder.

"I would love to, thank you."

Claro led them to a large 4x4 Toyota pickup truck. It was painted forest green and looked like one of those safari vehicles.

Claro got into the driver's seat. Dana rode shotgun. The back of the truck had two rows of seats for three people.

Ramón and Iris sat in the middle row. The back row was empty.

Claro fired up the engine. He shifted the gear into first and they were off and running.

It was a ten-minute drive that was absolutely stunning. Dana loved taking Big Red off-roading whenever she could, but her trips were bush league compared to what she was witnessing: rolling, green, lush hills.

"Most of the reserve is protected from human interference and accessible only for research or educational purposes," Claro explained as he drove.

"It's stunning here," Dana said.

"Doña Elsa ensured that the montane forest and alpine pastures you're looking at were protected. You're experiencing one of the best preserved montane ecosystems in the western hemisphere," Iris said from the backseat.

"Paradise," Claro said, beaming with pride.

He drove the truck down a steep hillside, crossing a creek, and then up the mountainside then back down again. Dana loved the rollercoaster ride as she looked down to a river in the distance as Claro drove towards it.

"That's Río Bello," Ramón said.

"Río Bello is a tributary of the San Juan River that flows into the Caribbean Sea," Iris added.

Dana felt clueless with all these experts she was with. It was quite the eclectic mix. Iris the Swedish Ph.D. candidate in biodiversity studies, and Claro and Ramón self-taught locals who seemed to know just as much as the doctoral candidate when it came to the breathtaking mountain ecosystem they were in.

Claro drove up to the river and parked. "We hike the rest of the way," he told Dana.

The group hiked through the forest for about twenty

minutes until they arrived at their destination. "There they are," Ramón said in awe.

Even before Ramón had spoken, Dana had already spotted the cornucopia of beautifully colored orchids that were gently swaying in the warm, wet breeze of the rainforest.

"Stunning," Dana said. It dawned on her that that was about all she could muster to say since she climbed onto the truck.

They walked closer to the wild orchids.

"What you're seeing right there can't be found anywhere else in the country," Claro said.

"Those flowers are as rare as they come," Iris said, confirming what Claro had said.

"And these are valuable to scientists?" Dana asked.

"Oh yeah. These would have all been long gone had it not been for Doña Elsa's preservation work," Iris said.

"Can you even put a monetary value to something as beautiful as this?" Dana asked as she took in the beautiful field of orchids.

"Depends. Some pharmaceutical companies believe those orchids are the gateway to millions of dollars in profit. Maybe billions," Iris explained forebodingly.

Dana turned away from the orchids to face Iris. She was speaking metaphorically. She wasn't expecting Iris to put a price tag, especially one in the millions like that.

"Seriously?"

"It's a big business. It costs a fortune in research for a pharmaceutical company to reap in the big money, but it can all start with an orchid, just like that one," Iris said, pointing at a pretty white orchid.

"That is why Doña Elsa was very picky about the research programs she partnered with, and she didn't like exclusive agreements, which made some of the program managers upset, so she just wouldn't work with them," Claro added.

"I had no idea that orchids could be sought after for those types of purposes. I just thought they were pretty to look at." She couldn't help but think that the reserve's land was valuable for developers and now she was learning some of the wildflowers, in particular the orchids, could be just as valuable. Doña Elsa was sitting on a fortune and she didn't seem to care that she could wring cash from the reserve. She might not have cared, but maybe someone else did. And the best way to get their hands on the orchids was by getting rid of Elsa and Eladio.

## CHAPTER TWELVE

THE NEXT DAY MAX PERRY TEXTED DANA BACK.

"Sorry I missed you. I had to visit the US embassy in San José."

Dana texted him back: "Hope everything is OK."

"All is well, just some paperwork that needed to be done for one of my grants. You enjoy the tour?"

"I did. The orchids were stunning."

"Orchids?"

"Claro drove us to a field full of beautiful orchids by the river."

He didn't text back right away. Dana figured he got busy, so she grabbed her keys to head out to the market to pick up something for dinner. It was going to be a special dinner.

Benny was heading back to town that evening. And she was excited because he told her that he was going to spend a week in Mariposa Beach. His daughter was traveling to Miami with his ex-wife and he had a light workload that didn't require going to the courthouse or meeting with clients in the city. The only closing he had was for a retired American couple that bought a beach house nearby in Sámara. Since all he needed was his laptop and an Internet connection, he would work from his home in Mariposa Beach.

Benny lived in the opposite direction of Casa Verde, but the town was tiny, so he was going to be a ten-minute drive away versus the four hours from San José.

They decided to spend the evening at Casa Verde wining, dining, netflixing, and chilling.

THE SUPER FRESCO was located right next door from Ark Row. It was a small grocery store, but the owner, Jerónimo Uribe—whom everyone called Jerry—was a savvy grocer who catered to the tourists and expats in town and their froufrou food shopping needs. Dana was surprised when she first visited Jerry's store because it reminded her of a small Whole Foods with its organic items down to the *whole paycheck* high prices to boot. But the quality of Jerry's food and produce was always top notch and well worth the prices. Especially since it all had to be schlepped all the way down to the coast.

DANA CAME BACK from the supermarket forty minutes later excited to cook up the dinner plan she had in mind: spaghetti alla carbonara with pancetta topped with parmesan cheese. She loved the local cuisine, but she missed Italian food, so when she saw that the Fresh Market had pancetta—an item that the small grocery store in Mariposa Beach didn't usually carry—she saw it as a sign that tonight would be pasta night.

She was opening up a bottle of red wine from Napa Valley that her best friend in San Francisco, Courtney Lowe, had given her when she last visited Mariposa Beach when she received a text.

She assumed it was from Benny, but it was from Max. She had forgotten that they had been texting until he stopped responding.

"Did you find anything interesting about the orchids?"

"That they're beautiful. Also apparently very valuable for scientists doing research. Had no clue," Dana texted back.

"Who told you that? A student or Ramón? They don't know what they're talking about."

*Okay, that's rude,* Dana thought, wondering why he was texting that. She imagined he was under a lot of stress with having to find a new place for his research and to complete his doctorate with the reserve being in limbo, so she shrugged it off as stress and decided to share the good news about their plans to protect the orchids. She texted him back about that, ignoring the snide comments:

"Claro and Ramón are meeting with Elsa to ensure the orchids and other rare flowers are protected from developers that are circling around like vultures."

She expected him to text back excitedly and offer to help with the project, but instead he went dark. Once again Dana shrugged it off. Besides, she had to finish making dinner. She didn't want to mess up dinner, since Benny was the one usually cooking delicious dinners for them. She looked at the clock on the microwave and yelped. Benny would arrive soon, so she needed to shove the dinner-making process into high gear.

Wally wasn't helping; he kept getting in her way underfoot as he circled by her feet, waiting to snap up any delicious morsel she might drop onto the floor. She was amused how fast he was —dog-like—when it came up to snapping up goodies that fell to the floor. He was like a furry Roomba vacuum.

Dana was chopping up some broccoli when a stray floret

went airborne and tumbled to the ground. Wally pounced on it like a tiger in the Serengeti. He spit out the green vegetable from his mouth and looked up at Dana in utter disgust and disdain, demanding she drop some pancetta, not the green disgusting stuff.

She laughed. "Hey, not everything that I drop is a piece of meat," she said, looking down at Wally. He just sat there staring up at her. *If looks could kill.*

BENNY ARRIVED BRANDISHING DESSERT, tres leches cake. They were going to have a feast worth going into a food coma afterwards.

She poured two glasses of wine and served up the pasta on two plates. Benny took the plates and set them on the dining room table.

"I'll get the utensils," he said, darting back into the kitchen as Dana headed over to the table with the two glasses of wine.

He handed her a spoon and a fork. She smiled. They ate the pasta the Italian way. He used the spoon to twirl the pasta onto his fork and put it into his mouth.

"This is delicious," Benny said after his first bite of the meal.

"You sound surprised," Dana said with a grin.

"Well, I mean, I didn't mean to imply..." Dana let Benny stutter for another moment before she broke out in laughter.

"I don't cook often, but I can cook when I set my mind to it and I have a recipe I can follow," Dana said.

As they ate, Benny filled in Dana with what he had been up to the past five days. His law practice focused on real estate law, but he also did what he called expat law: immigration and residency work for mostly North Americans from the United States and Canada.

Dana told Benny how she went up to the reserve with Ramón and finally got the tour of the reserve from Claro Madderra, since Max Perry was MIA.

"They said those orchids are very valuable, not just as a beautiful flower but for research scientists."

"For medicinal purposes?" Benny asked.

"That's what Claro said. But he said Elsa wasn't interested in letting big pharma have access to her land unless it was for non-profit or a university. She also wasn't keen to develop some beauty products like anti-aging creams or diet pills that would make dubious claims. And that seemed to be the type of companies interested in her orchids."

"Anti-aging cream? They have that?" Benny asked, laughing.

"It's a great marketing scheme to say a cream can stop the aging process," Dana scoffed. "It's a bit sad. Doña Elsa preferred to work with universities, which helped stave off the pharma money, and now that she's been arrested they're all cutting ties and recalling their students even though she hasn't even been charged with a crime yet. It's too bad the universities are not supporting her right now when she needs it the most."

"The business side of a university can be just as cold hearted as a corporation. They have to protect their own business interests. They're not going to stick around or stand by her if parents are freaking out that they sent their kids to a reserve where its owner has been arrested for murder that happened at the reserve their kids are staying in."

"They're doing just that," Dana said, bringing the wine glass up to her lips and taking a sip.

"You still haven't heard from Max Perry?"

"He texted today. He seems stressed."

"You could deduct that from a text message?" Benny asked, grinning.

"Sure, you can glean plenty from the written word. He didn't seem too happy that I was at the reserve looking at those orchids and that Ramón had been talking with Elsa about bringing the rare orchids here to keep them safe."

"Sounds like everyone is on edge. A murder. Doña Elsa arrested. The future of the reserve in question. It must be tough all around for everyone at the reserve," Benny said.

"That's why Ramón wants to plant those orchids here, to ensure they're not lost in the chaos going on up there."

"You can do that? Dig up a plant and replant it somewhere else?"

Dana laughed. "I asked the same question. Ramón says he can do it. If anyone can do it, I believe Ramón can. You look up 'green thumb' in the dictionary and you'll find his picture next to the definition."

Benny chuckled then asked, "Was Claro okay with that?"

"He was, but he said it wasn't his decision to make and that Ramón needed to ask Elsa, which is a bit of a challenge with her sitting in jail."

"All of this is so surreal," Benny said.

"It is. I need a sugar fix. Tres leches time," Dana said, eyeing the delicious creamy cake sitting on the kitchen's center island, beckoning her.

# CHAPTER THIRTEEN

Dana arrived at the bookstore slash cafe at eight a.m. with Wally in toe. Wally had been homeless when he made his way to Dana's veranda, so he was not one to be put in a carry-on kennel. Instead, she would plop him on the passenger side of Big Red. He seemed to love the fresh air when the top was down, and he would look at the world, not seeming scared of the bumpy car ride down to the bookstore. He was a smart cat, so she didn't worry about him jumping out to chase after something. She parked and looked over at Wally, who was standing on his hind legs looking out the window.

"I swear you were a dog in a past life," Dana said, scratching him behind his left ear.

Dana walked into her store with Wally in her arms. As usual, Amalfi had opened shop, and Mindy and Leo were minding the cafe side of the store.

The bookstore side of the business didn't officially open until nine a.m., but if one of Mindy's customers wanted to buy a book, Amalfi was there helping with the morning rush, so she would take off her barista apron and put on her book-selling one. She was a godsend that allowed Dana to be more of a landlord and absent owner when she was running around doing this or that.

It was a strange arrangement, but Dana and Mindy were friends and they trusted each other, so it worked.

Dana put Wally down, who made his way to his favorite spot by the large window facing Main Street. Dana had put a kitty condo in front of the window next to the book display rack. The sun drenched that spot all morning and most of the afternoon, much to Wally's delight. He could soak in the sunlight and people-watch the passersby. Dana and Amalfi just had to keep an eye on him to ensure he didn't try to raid the goodies that Leo kept in the kitchen to make his bagel sandwiches. The tuna, salmon, and bacon were his favorite heist targets.

On that morning, the buzz from the entire hullabaloo surrounding Doña Elsa from the last few days was subsiding, and it seemed like Mariposa Beach was settling back into its regular routine.

It was earlier than usual for Dana to be at the bookstore, but she didn't want to miss out on any of the talk about the case. However, the gossip had moved on from Dona Elsa and her murdered husband to an American tourist in his sixties with his twenty-something-year-old girlfriend. He seemed to get more disgust from the Gossip Brigade than a suspected murderer.

Mindy smiled wide at her when she had walked into the store earlier than usual. Dana blushed, knowing that Mindy knew why she was there early.

She thought about saying something about how she needed to do some inventory or something along those lines, but she figured it was a silly thing to lie about, so she shrugged her shoulders and smiled back in acknowledgment. *I know you know why I'm here early.*

She went to her office. Wally jumped off from his condo perch and followed her into the office. "You can hang out by the window," Dana said, but he ignored her. He waltzed inside and jumped on her desk, circled a couple times, and plopped on some paperwork she was planning to go over. "Of course," Dana said, shaking her head.

She dreamed that Wally would be the perfect bookstore cat. But he never really took to it. He would run off or hiss when customers would pet him. She thought of Joe Pesci as Tommy DeVito from *Goodfellas* staring back at a customer, hissing, "What? I'm here to amuse you?"

Eventually he would get bored and bolt out the door to have fun roaming out about town. She had given up trying to make a former stray outdoor cat into an indoor cat. He always made his way back home, and that's all that mattered to her. She had really become attached to the furry little stinker.

Dana sat down and looked at the security cameras on her computer monitor. There were a few customers in line to place an order at the cafe, and a couple people were perusing the bookshelves. The romance and mystery sections were the most popular.

It struck Dana how quickly people move on when something doesn't directly impact them. The murder occurred at the reserve, which was way up the mountain, miles away. Life quickly went back to normal on the beach.

She imagined the Gossip Brigade was around their usual table overlooking the ocean at the Qué Vista Restaurant, where they would be kibitzing as usual while playing a card game.

Meanwhile, Doña Elsa sat in jail and the reserve was circling down the drain.

Dana wished there was something she could do, but there wasn't anything to do but let the wheels of justice keep turning, even if it was at a frustratingly glacier pace. The US legal system moved slowly, but in Costa Rica it moved even slower.

Just about every aspect of living in Costa Rica was slower

compared to the fast-paced life in the States. It was why many expats like herself moved down but then were struck by just how slow everything was in comparison. But you have to respect that way of life. Grin and bear it and chuck it off as life in the tropics.

She wondered if there was anything she could do to help Doña Elsa, but she wasn't keen about sticking her nose in yet another police investigation. It was the last thing she needed to do in her life after several unpleasant dealings with Detective Jorge Picado.

She focused on her work at hand by trying to wedge an invoice from underneath Wally's comatose body when she heard someone yell, "Holy cow, come look at this, it's him!"

She got up and made her way back into the cafe. It sounded like it was Leo, but that couldn't be. He was usually cool as a cucumber, and she had never seen him raise his voice like that. She made her way to the front of the bookstore slash cafe. She was halfway through the store when she saw Leo rushing out of the kitchen, shouting once again saying, "Holy cow."

"What is it? Did you cut yourself again?" Mindy asked, inspecting his hands.

"No, I didn't cut myself," Leo said, sounding offended at the question.

"What's up?" Dana asked.

"It's him. On the TV," he said excitedly.

"Who?" Mindy and Dana asked in unison.

"That jerk that was in here the other day giving you lip about the cream cheese," he replied, looking at Mindy.

"The guy that got mad because we were out of the mango cream cheese?" Mindy asked.

"Yes, him. The jerk," Leo said.

Unfortunately, in the food and retail business, you needed

more clues to hone down on a particular difficult customer, since many of them came in all spades of jerkiness.

"What's he doing on the TV?" Dana asked.

"He's on the news. He's been arrested at the airport," Leo said.

Dana figured he must have been accused of doing something pretty bad to make the television news.

"Wow, what did he do?" she asked.

"He probably got kicked off his flight for berating the flight attendant because they didn't have the booze he wanted," Mindy snarked.

"Nothing like that. Worse, actually. Smuggling," Leo said.

"Oh my gosh, drugs?" Dana asked.

"No. It's weird, actually. He was trying to smuggle wild flowers out of the country," Leo said.

"Flowers?" Mindy was confused.

"Well, not just regular flowers. According to the news, he was trying to smuggle out flowers that are on the list of the endangered species of flora. A big no-no."

Dana physically reeled in shock. She felt lightheaded. She looked at Mindy and knew they were thinking the same thing.

"Do you think this has anything to do with the wildflower reserve here?" Mindy asked Dana.

"That's what I'm wondering. He was down here and he seemed very interested in the reserve, and then I saw him talking with Max Perry a few times," Dana said.

"The reserve has protected flowers?" asked Amalfi, who had been listening with curiosity.

"It sure does. I was just there yesterday. Ramón is trying to save some rare orchids that only grow there. He seems to think he can get them to grow on my property, but needs to go through a whole process to get permission. And one of the graduate students said those orchids could hold the key to a multimillion-dollar Botox cream for a lucky pharmaceutical company," Dana replied.

"You really think he was trying to smuggle flowers he got from the reserve back to the States?" Leo asked. He didn't sound convinced.

"I have no idea. I'm just thinking it's all very strange and a big coincidence if it's not related," Dana said, sounding ominous.

"We'll find out soon enough," Leo said, trying to get back to work.

"I'm going to do a little online research," Dana said.

"Uh-oh," Mindy said, knowing that when Dana's curiosity was piqued, sometimes all heck could break loose.


DANA WENT BACK to her back office. Wally was gone, having left fur-fuzz on her paperwork. *Little bugger*, she thought. She warned Leo that Wally was MIA.

"Lock up the bacon."

"He better not try to raid my kitchen again," he said forebodingly.

"Relax, honey, he wanted to go outside so I let him out," Mindy said.

With that mystery solved, Dana went back into her office. She wanted to watch the video news coverage that Leo had watched, so she had to go find it online.

She sat down, placing the laptop on the desk and opening it. She waited for a few seconds for it to connect to the cafe's WIFI network: *BookandJavaJunkies*.

Although Mariposa Beach was rural, the Internet connection speeds were very good—which had surprised her, since she had visited other developing countries where the Internet wasn't as good or reliable.

Dana fired up the Chrome browser and went to the Teletica News website. Teletica Canal 7 was the first television station in Costa Rica when it started up in 1960. Their news program remains one of the most respected in the country.

It took her a few minutes of clicking around the website to find the video clip. It didn't seem that rare-flower smuggling was considered too big of a news story, since it was buried deep down in the website.

But she found it. She clicked play on the video and watched with interest as agents with OIJ emblazoned jackets escorted the loudmouth from the airport terminal to a waiting car. He was handcuffed. He ignored the reporter's request for comment, instead giving her an icy glare and keeping his mouth shut.

The news reporter referred to him as an American citizen from Massachusetts. His name was Curt Bennett. The reporter also mentioned, just as Leo had informed her, that Bennett was smuggling protected flora and that an anonymous person had tipped off the police. That's all the information they had, so Dana had no idea if he had gotten the flowers from the reserve or somewhere else in the country. She didn't even know what kind of flowers he was trying to smuggle out or why. For all she knew he just liked flowers and was sneaking some back home to plant them in his backyard.

Items that don't seem to be a big deal to bring back home, like flowers, or dirt, a handful of sand from the beach, a sea shell, or even just visiting a farm with animal stock were of concern for customs officials worldwide, which is why what you take out or bring into countries is monitored and controlled by governments all over the world.

Costa Rica is no exception. The country has a good reputation for its conservation efforts, and the United States Department of Agriculture has strict rules that restrict or prohibit the entry of many agricultural products, which can carry foreign pests and diseases that harm American agriculture and the local environment.

That is why travelers are asked to declare all the agricultural products you are bringing with you. If you lie about it or try to sneak it into the country without declaring it, that traveler could face serious penalties and even prison time.

It's a serious business on both sides of the coin. Both the Costa Rican and US authorities worry about what you're trying to take out or bring into the country.

*But what was Curt Bennet up to?* Dana wondered as she began Googling for information about Curt Bennett.

She struck Google gold right away on page one, where she found a link to Curt Bennett's LinkedIn page. She clicked on the link and the page loaded. Dana's eyes darted quickly through the profile.

The profile photograph matched the loudmouth that was in the bookstore slash cafe a few days ago and the man arrested at the airport; there was no doubt this was the same person.

She kept on reading his profile, scrolling down through his bio, and she froze. She could feel her jaw dropping as she read the man's profile description. She read it twice to make sure she wasn't seeing things.

The loudmouth that was such a jerk at the bookstore slash cafe, the man arrested at the airport—Curt Bennett—had over twenty years of experience working in the pharmaceutical industry, the last six years as a self-employed independent consultant.

Dana toggled back to the browser's tab for the news channel's website and she clicked on the video of Curt Bennett's arrest at the airport. She sat back on her chair, watching the video again. "What were you up to down here, Mr. Bennet?" Dana asked out loud, even though she was alone in her office.

# CHAPTER FOURTEEN

EARLY IN THE MORNING, BENNY GOT READY TO DRIVE UP TO the capital. He had several closings lined up and a legal brief to file with the court, so he would be gone for a few days. They had spent a lovely week together, but he had to get back home. The only thing that excited him about going back to the city was to see his daughter.

"I'll be back on Friday night with Beatrice," Benny said.

Dana had forgotten this was his weekend with his daughter.

"Oh, that's great, I'm looking forward to seeing her," she said.

Dana didn't want to impose on the time between father and daughter, but she had become fond of the girl and they got along well—much to her relief, since the odds of a tween girl warming up to her dad's girlfriend were stacked up high against the new girlfriend.

Benny smiled and kissed Dana gently on the lips. They hugged and he got into his SUV and drove off.

Dana stood by her front door, watching him drive away as the SUV made its way down her long driveway, leaving back a dust trail that made her feel sad. She felt like a sailor's girlfriend standing at the pier sending her man off to sea. "Snap out of it, silly," Dana said to herself. He would be back in a few days. But she couldn't help feeling melancholic. She wasn't a fan of the long-distance relationship.

She was about to go back inside for a second cup of coffee when she saw Ramón walking up from his place towards the grove of trees on the south side of the property. He was holding a weed whacker in one hand, with his trusty machete dangling from its brown leather sheath by his hip as usual.

She waved and called his name. He smiled and changed directions, walking towards her.

"Good morning, Doña Dana," he said, smiling.

"Morning, Ramón. What are you up to?"

"I was going to work on the avocado trees and the yuca roots before it gets too hot," he said, looking up at the sky.

"Have you had a chance to visit Doña Elsa in jail to see how she's doing and to see if she's okay with you taking some of her orchids to replant here?" Dana asked.

"Not yet," he said, sounding guilty that he hadn't gone there yet.

"I was wondering if I could go with you? I'd like to talk to her."

Ramón looked surprised. "Sure. I don't think that would be a problem."

"Maybe we can go this morning? When you're ready, of course," Dana said.

Ramón's eyes lit up. "That would be great," he said.

She figured part of the reason he hadn't made the trip to the Nicoya jail yet was that he didn't want to go there alone. She knew that his wife, Carmen, didn't want to go, saying she was scared of jail visits. Dana understood. People had real phobias about visiting a jail.

"Okay then. I'll have some breakfast and shower. Can you be ready in an hour?"

"Sure," Ramón said. "The weeding can wait until another day."

BACK INSIDE THE HOUSE, Dana ate avocado toast with a glass of orange juice. Both the avocado and the oranges came from her property, which she swore made it even more delicious and special.

She took a bite of the toast and avocado as Wally watched. He sniffed the air, getting a whiff of the green fruit on her toast, then he walked away in disgust. Dana laughed, figuring he was upset that she wasn't having bacon and eggs for breakfast.

"Snob," she said as he sauntered away.

After breakfast, she poured another cup of coffee and went upstairs to shower.

As she showered, she couldn't stop thinking about Curt Bennett, Max Perry, Doña Elsa, and those orchids. She wasn't sure what her master plan was by inviting herself to visit Doña Elsa. She hadn't even met the woman and had only seen her that one time during the chaotic aftermath of her husband's murder. But she wanted to know if she knew Curt Bennett.

Was he in town to try to get her to sell him her rare orchids? And why would Max Perry be talking to him and then become obtuse when she mentioned Ramón's plan to work with Claro to save Doña Elsa's orchids? As a botanist who was on his way out of the country, she would think he would be pleased that those rare orchids were being taken care of after he was gone.

Ramón was waiting by Big Red. He had taken off his gray long-sleeve blended twill coverall which he wore every day, and had on a red polo shirt tucked into his blue jeans. He was also wearing white sneakers.

She smiled. She wasn't used to seeing him dressed casually in his street clothes.

"Ready?" she asked him. He nodded. "Let's go, then," Dana said, climbing into the driver's seat. He sat in the passenger seat and held onto the door frame grips.

"I don't drive that bad," Dana said, laughing.

Ramón blushed. "Not bad, just a little too fast," he said, embarrassed.

"I'll keep it under a hundred," she said with a snicker as she fired up Big Red. He looked at her wide-eyed. "Just kidding," she said as she backed out of her carport, turning wide so she could turn the Jeep around so it was facing in the right direction. She pressed on the accelerator as they made their way down her driveway.

It was an hour's drive from Mariposa Beach up to the closest OIJ substation in Nicoya, where Doña Elsa was jailed until she was sent to Costa Rica's only women's prison, El Buen Pastor. From there she would have to wait to be charged and for her trial to eventually start.

The OIJ station in Nicoya was of the national Judicial Police, the OIJ. In Costa Rica, the national police force is tasked with preventing crime and enforcing the law. The OIJ agents like Picado and Rojas are in charge of investigating crimes committed. It made the judicial process burdensome for far-flung beach towns like Mariposa Beach. Even petty crime, like a stolen cell phone, means having to file a denunciation—an official police complaint—with the OIJ in Nicoya. A citizen can't do that with the police force. So you would have to drive all the way up to Nicoya to file a police report even if the uniformed police officer was first on the scene or their police stations were closer to Mariposa Beach. It didn't matter. If you wanted to file a criminal complaint, you had to trek all the way up to Nicoya. It was a real pain, and it meant most petty crimes went unreported.

On the drive up, Dana and Ramón talked mostly about Doña Elsa and those rare orchids.

It became even more apparent what a big role Doña Elsa had played in Ramón's formative life.

"When I was a boy, I worked at the reserve. I learned everything I know about plants and gardening from Doña Elsa," he said wistfully.

"Do you know anything about those orchids being valuable to pharmaceutical companies?" Dana asked.

"Oh, sure, they're always coming around. But I don't know how much money they offered her, if any. They just wanted the orchids so they could figure out how to get them to grow in a lab. They don't care about the actual flower and whether or not it continues to grow in the wild, naturally. They just want to harness its goodness into something they can charge an arm and a leg for."

"Is it easy to get them to grow in a lab?"

"No. I can't even guarantee that I can get those orchids to grow on your land. It's why they are so rare. They seem to be very picky about the soil and the right conditions. Not too much shade or sun. Not too much water. Orchids are very persnickety. They love the soil of the reserve. I also believe the orchids love Doña Elsa. There is a reason people talk to plants. They respond to that kind of positive energy. They won't respond to white coats in a lab," Ramón said.

Having grown up in the city, Dana didn't know much about gardening, but she had heard plants respond to people. It was a strange concept for her to wrap her head around, but it was obvious that Ramón believed in it wholeheartedly.

They made it into Nicoya and she drove directly to the police station, which made Dana nervous. She was walking into Detective Jorge Picado's domain, and the last thing she wanted to do was run into the surly detective.

## CHAPTER FIFTEEN

THE JUDICIAL POLICE STATION WAS BUSTLING INSIDE. IT emanated a drab impersonal and unwelcoming aura. Not that Dana had a lot of experience in police stations, but most civilians don't go there for fun, so there is that feel of despair in the air, which she didn't like one bit.

She and Ramón walked up to the reception area, where there was a young woman with long, raven-black hair sitting there. Dana didn't know if she was a policewoman or a civilian employee, but she seemed nice enough.

"How can I help you?" she asked with a smile.

"We're here to visit a friend," Ramón said.

Dana looked around. There were several men and women in police uniforms with their guns in their holsters and others dressed in regular clothing—business casual style—who were also armed, with their badges dangling from a chain around their neck. She recognized them as being the special agents of the OIJ, the Judicial Police—the equivalent of police detectives back in America. She knew this from her interactions with OIJ agents Jorge Picado and Gabriela Rojas, then she shuddered, thinking she might run into Picado and how he would probably hit the roof seeing her interfering in another of his cases. Not that she was interfering. She was just there to help Ramón save Doña Elsa's orchids.

"What's your friend's name?" the young woman asked Ramón.

"Elsa Calderón."

Dana had forgotten Elsa's full name, since everyone just referred to her as Doña Elsa.

The girl tapped on the computer. She kept her fingernails short and they were painted in a dark brown color as she tapped away. Dana was impressed with her fast typing skills. Figured she must be a front desk-type receptionist. Most cops she had met typed in the hunt-and-peck mode.

She was typing away for a while. "There are visiting hours, right?" Ramón asked nervously.

"Sure thing," the receptionist replied without looking up from her computer monitor.

After about a minute of looking at the computer, she turned her attention back to Ramón and Dana. "I'll need your cédulas, please."

The cédula was the Costa Rican national identification card that every Costa Rican citizen must carry. It's similar to a Social Security number, but the cédula number isn't kept securely like in the United States. In Costa Rica, the cédula is used more like a driver's license or a state-issued ID card, used just about anywhere an ID is needed, like at a grocery store or at the bank.

Since Dana was an expat, she didn't have a cédula ID card issued, so she brought her US passport for identification.

The receptionist looked at Dana with raised eyebrows but then smiled as she took her passport and Ramón's cédula.

"One moment, please," she said, taking the IDs and turning her attention back to her computer. After another minute, she gave them back their IDs and asked them to take a seat in the waiting room until their name was called.

They thanked her and went to the so-called waiting room that the receptionist had pointed out to them. It wasn't really a room but several lines of orange plastic chairs in the middle of the building. It reminded Dana more like the waiting area at an airport. There were several other people sitting there, like a young couple with a child. He was dressed like a hip hop star wannabe and she was dressed in tight Daisy Duke shorts that made Dana squirm, thinking how uncomfortable it must be walking around in that getup. She doubted the couple was even twenty years of age. Their toddler was adorable, but he was left to run around the police station unchecked. There were a couple of men with hard faces and mean eyes which made Dana uncomfortable. There were also a couple of campesinos and a couple old ladies with sad eyes. Dana imagined they were there to visit their friends and family who were in jail.

The cells here were just holding cells, so it didn't have the sense of complete dread that you have visiting a real prison. Dana had visited plenty of those back when she was a journalist in California, including the state's only death row prison, San Quentin in Northern California. The surroundings here reminded Dana of San Quentin. It looked old and crumbling.

They sat there for about ten minutes, chatting about the weather and how uncomfortable they felt being there.

"A good reminder to stay on the right side of the law," Ramón said with a smile.

Dana agreed wholeheartedly.

"Villalobos. Kirkpatrick," Dana heard someone shout out their names. Her last name was pronounced as *Keerkpatreek*, which was just about the way all the locals pronounced it, since Kirkpatrick was a rare last name in Costa Rica. She was getting used to it.

"Here," she said as she and Ramón got up from the uncomfortable plastic chairs.

They walked up to the uniformed police offer holding a piece of paper in his hand.

"Good morning," Dana said to the young officer, who ignored her, not bothering to greet her back.

"Cédulas," he barked instead.

Ramón pulled out his Velcro wallet and again dug out his ID as Dana did the same, pulling out her passport from her purse.

The police officer checked them out against a piece of paper he held in his free hand. He grunted and handed back their IDs.

"Follow me," he said as he turned back and headed towards the rear of the building.

They walked through a sea of plastic orange chairs which then gave way to a sea of desks with scores of men and women sitting working away, most of them peeking up at them from their computers. Dana noticed some of them had handguns in holsters on their hips, while others weren't armed, or at least not that she could tell.

The police officer that hadn't introduced himself so he was nameless kept walking on a brisk pace with Ramón and Dana trying to keep up behind him.

He led them to a door that had a placard on it that read: VISITANTES          AUTORIZADOS—AUTHORIZED VISITORS.

He opened the door and inside was a small windowless conference room. There was a small table with three chairs. Two on one side and the third on the other side of the table.

"Sit there," the police officer pointed at the two chairs next to each other.

Ramón and Dana did as they were told.

"Wait here," he said before he walked out, closing the door.

"He's a friendly guy," Dana said, grinning, which made Ramón laugh out loud. She joined him. It was a welcome break from the tense atmosphere they found themselves in.

There was a big clock on the wall and two security cameras, but that was it for decor.

The clock was one of those high school clocks that tracked time down to the second, with a thin clock hand ticking every second. After a while in silence, the moving seconds hand of the clock sounded like a jackhammer every time it ticked off a second. Her back was to the door, which made the waiting feel more anxious as she kept cranking her neck over her shoulder to see if anyone was standing back there. Ramón just sat quietly, his arms on the table. She was a fidgety mess. It was always hard for her to wait around quietly, especially if she was nervous, and being at the police station knowing that Picado might be out there roaming the hallways made her more nervous, even though her criminal record in her entire life consisted of two speeding tickets. But we won't get into parking tickets. She was a regular Al Capone when it came to the world of illegal parking in San Francisco.

She sat there for what felt like hours, her attention drawn to that darn clock. But in reality they only had to wait a few minutes until they heard the doorknob jangle.

# CHAPTER SIXTEEN

THE DOOR WAS FLUNG OPEN AS DANA TURNED AROUND TO see the police officer escort Doña Elsa into the room. She wasn't handcuffed, which surprised Dana. She wore a gray jumpsuit.

"Ramón, I'm so happy to see you," she said as she hugged him.

This also surprised Dana, since in the States there were strict rules about having physical contact with prisoners, especially one suspected of murder. Usually the visitor sat behind a bulletproof glass, only able to communicate with the jailed person from a phone.

"You have thirty minutes. Not one second more," the dour policeman said as he closed the door and left them all alone. Dana figured they were being watched via the security cameras mounted on the wall, but it still surprised Dana that they were left alone.

It made her relax a little, since the crabby police officer added to the already uncomfortable tension of visiting someone behind bars.

It was a surreal experience, visiting someone who, unlike Dana and Ramón, couldn't just walk out of this room. She was under arrest. And since there is no American bail bond system in Costa Rica, she couldn't bond out to await trial at home. She was under preventive detention, and she could be held there for months while the prosecutors and the OIJ put together their case against her.

Unlike the United States, in Costa Rica, you weren't innocent until proven guilty. It was literally the other way around; you were guilty until proven innocent.

The Costa Rican criminal law system follows the European-Continental tradition. Unlike in the United States, there is no jury system here. A trial is presided over by a single judge or by a three-judge panel, depending on the crime. Since this was a murder charge, Doña Elsa would have to face a three-judge panel once she was put on trial, and they would decide her fate.

Not that the trial would be happening anytime soon. Although she could be held on pre-trial detention for one year, that still meant she could sit in jail for one year without even being charged or going on trial. And prosecutors could have that extended if the court agreed more time was needed.

And although she could not be held in detention longer than twenty-four hours without a court order, that ship had sailed for Doña Elsa, since she had now been held here for days since they arrested her. Dana assumed the court order had been issued. If Doña Elsa was truly innocent, she could spend up to a year in jail and not even spend a day in court.

It made Dana's stomach ache thinking about that as she saw the grandmotherly-looking person in front of her. That's when she noticed that Doña Elsa was looking at her curiously.

"So you're the new owner of Casa Verde. Ramón speaks highly of you," Doña Elsa said, smiling.

Dana smiled awkwardly. "Yes, I am. It's nice to meet you," she said, holding her hand out then feeling foolish for doing that.

Doña Elsa smiled and shook her hand.

"I knew your uncle. He was a good man. I'm sorry for your loss."

"Oh, thanks."

"Ramón told me you've been very kind to him and his family ever since you inherited Casa Verde from your uncle."

Dana blushed. "I would be lost without Ramón and Carmen," Dana said.

"Are they treating you well in here?" Ramón asked.

"Oh, yes, dear. They're kind to an old woman like myself. But I don't want to spend another second in here if it were up to me."

"I can't even imagine what you're going through," Dana said. And she couldn't even fathom. Her husband was dead and the police believed she killed him, so here she sat in jail while they prepared to try her for his murder. She was looking at a long prison sentence even though Costa Rica had much more lenient prison sentencing guidelines than the United States. There is no such thing as life in prison. And the most a person could be incarcerated for was fifty years. Benny had told Dana that Doña Elsa was looking at a twenty-year prison sentence, which at her age would be like a life sentence.

"I'm innocent, so I'm just trying to keep the faith that I'll be out of here soon," she said.

To Dana, she seemed to be trying to stay positive and strong, but there was a forlorn aura around her that caused Dana to choke back a tear. The next twenty minutes Ramón and Doña Elsa talked about the orchids. Dana sat back and watched them both talk about the flowers with such excitement that they beamed, and during those twenty minutes it didn't seem like they were talking in a conference room at the police station where Doña Elsa was being held. It's as if they were back in the reserve talking about a landscaping project. It was all about the orchids.

Doña Elsa walked Ramón step-by-step on what he needed to do to ensure that he could successfully transfer the rare orchids from the reserve to Dana's property. Ramón was enthralled listening to her talk as he eagerly wrote down notes on a well-worn notebook with a crumpled-up green cover. Dana couldn't help but look down at the notebook that seemed to fill up with handwritten notes and drawings. It looked like a journal, but Dana wasn't sure, since she had never seen Ramón with it until that day.

"It's my landscaping recipe book," Ramón said with a smile when he noticed her looking at his notebook. Dana blushed and smiled.

Dana was tasked with being the time keeper, since they only had thirty minutes to visit. She more than up for the task, since she couldn't help but obsessively stare at that pesky second hand lurching forward on that wall clock Click. Click. Click. She felt like the narrator in Edgar Allan Poe's "The Tell-Tale Heart" freaking out as the noise grew louder in her head. *What was that line from that story?* She tried to remember. *Ah, yes. Hark! louder! louder! louder! louder!*

She snapped out of her Poe and clock trance. "We have ten minutes left," Dana said.

The time check seemed to hit Doña Elsa like a nightmarish reality check. Talking with Ramón about her orchids took her back to her old life at the reserve. Dana felt bad. She wondered how she was processing the murder of her husband. The consensus was that he was a lout, but she stayed with him, so part of her might be devastated that he'd been killed. And she wasn't even able to process or deal with those emotions, since she was arrested for his murder so quickly.

Dana wasn't about to ask her about it, and Doña Elsa never mentioned her husband.

Dana asked Ramón if he had the information he needed. He said he did. So she removed a legal document that Benny had drafted for her. It was a simple document giving Ramón and Dana permission to remove the orchids from Doña Elsa's property and for her to be able to bring them onto her property to be planted there. She felt sheepish about asking her to sign it, but Benny had been adamant, telling her "good intentions don't work in the court of law, so if anything goes sideways, you need to be protected legally."

Dana showed Doña Elsa the one-page document then slid it across the table towards her. "I totally understand if you want your own lawyer to look at it before signing it," Dana said.

Doña Elsa put on her reading glasses and she took a look. She read it in silence for a minute, then sat back and said, "No. That won't be necessary." She picked up the pen Dana had placed on the table and signed it, smiling.

"We'll make sure to take care of your orchids," Dana said.

"Our orchids," Doña Elsa corrected her with a smile.

With only a few minutes left in their visit—which the police officer warned couldn't last a second longer than thirty minutes —Dana had to ask if Doña Elsa knew Curt Bennett, the loud-mouth arrested for smuggling flowers out of the country a couple days ago.

"Curt Bennett?" Doña Elsa asked, a puzzled look on her face. "I don't know him, who is he?"

She wasn't allowed to bring her purse or cell phone into the visiting room, which she suspected would happen, so she pulled out a piece of paper with Curt Bennett's photograph that she had printed from the online article about his arrest. She had it folded in fours, so she unfolded and laid it out on the table.

"Have you ever seen this man?" Dana asked.

Doña Elsa put her reading glasses back on and took a close look. Then she took off her glasses and held out the paper with her hand away from her face as she squinted at it. She shook her head.

"No. I've never seen him before. Who is he?"

Dana told her about Curt Bennet and his arrest.

"I've always had pharmaceutical reps come to the reserve once I posted a photograph of my orchids on the website. I don't know how they found it, but I wish I hadn't posted it to my Facebook page and website, because they've been annoying me for the past two years, but he's not one of them. I've never seen him before."

"How well do you trust Max Perry?"

"Max?" Doña Elsa said, sounding utterly confused at Dana's question.

"Well, I saw him talking to that man a couple times in town," Dana said, pointing to Curt Bennett's photograph.

"He's only been at the reserve for a few months, but he seemed lovely to me. Smart and a hard worker. He's a scientist who loves biodiversity; he wouldn't have been mixed up with someone like that." Doña Elsa pointed at Curt Bennett's photograph on the table with her chin.

Just then the door flung open and Mr. Cheerful, the policeman, was back. "Time is up. Let's go," he said. All three of them got up from their chairs and Ramón and Dana took turns hugging Doña Elsa.

"Now," the policeman barked. A female police officer entered the room and took Doña Elsa away.

# CHAPTER SEVENTEEN

LATER THAT NIGHT, BACK AT HOME, DANA WAS VIDEO chatting with Benny on WhatsApp. She filled him in about visiting Doña Elsa and their excitement about trying to save the orchids.

"Did she sign the document I gave you?" Benny asked.

"She did without hesitation."

"She didn't want to have her lawyer review it?"

"Nope. She's just happy we're willing to look after her orchids."

"Good. I know you're doing this with your heart in the right place, but even actions made with good intentions can turn into nasty legal battles, especially since she has an estranged son and if those orchids are that valuable. The land alone is worth a pretty penny, so you I suspect a lot of lawyers will be sniffing around the reserve before Doña Elsa's legal problems are resolved."

"I understand. I do trust her, though, and she is the sole owner of the property, at least."

"Things are never that black and white when it comes to the law. We don't know what we don't know. She could have agreed to sell the orchids or license them or lease her land. Who knows what."

"She wouldn't do that. I'm sure she would have told us if she had done something like that."

"When Ray Kroc bought the rights to franchise McDonald's from the McDonald brothers, they failed to tell him they had already sold the rights to franchise to a few others. Ended up costing Krock a lot of money to resolve that. So you just never know what can be lurking out there. That document protected you."

Dana smiled. She trusted people, but Benny, as a lawyer, was trained to be cautious in these types of dealings. And she was glad he was looking out for her well-being, since these were possible issues that would have never crossed her mind.

"I know, and I am grateful. Even if I don't seem to, I really do appreciate your help with this stuff. You have saved my butt many times when it comes to legal shenanigans."

"When are you planning to get those orchids?"

"First thing in the morning."

"I wish you would wait until I'm there so I could come along."

"That's sweet, but we figured we need to get those orchids as soon as possible, especially if there are Curt Bennett types out there sniffing around like you said. I'll be fine, and Ramón and his cousin will be there too."

The next twenty minutes they chatted about Benny's day and how they missed each other and couldn't wait until the weekend when he would be back in town. They said their good-nights and Dana went to bed with Wally curled up by her head. She missed Benny. She began to drift into sleep as the howler monkeys began to serenade her with their loud grunts. She was used to them now, like folks who live by a train track. She fell asleep with a smile on her face.

THE NEXT MORNING, Dana was up at six a.m. She went for a thirty-minute run from her house down to the beach. She reached the rock formation that served as Mother Nature's barrier wall that divided Mariposa Beach from Piedra Chica Beach, which was the next town over. Piedra Chica meant "small rock" in Spanish, and the name fit it like a glove. The sand was littered with tiny sea rocks and shells that actually made it very difficult to walk on its sand barefoot, which is one of the reasons why Piedra Chica Beach was usually deserted in comparison to the other popular beaches that dotted the Pacific Coast of Costa Rica.

From this vantage point, the only way to go from Mariposa Beach to Piedra Chica Beach was up and over the rock formation, and only when the tide was low, so Dana always turned back from this point and ran back to town.

That spot also had bad memories for Dana. It was here that she had found a dead body a few months ago. And it was at that very rock formation that the killer had attacked her. Luckily she was able to get away and it all worked out in the end with the killer sent to prison. But the memories lingered. Still, she refused to let them control her life, so she made it a point to go on with her life like it was before, which included running to the rock formation. The more she did it, the quicker those bad memories faded to the background.

She made it back home drenched in sweat and sea splash. Even though it was early, the air was already muggy. But it wasn't warm enough for the air conditioner just yet, so she had all the windows open. The cool breeze from the Pacific mixed nicely with the breeze coming down from the mountains. Her property was built in the perfect spot to take advantage of those refreshing cross-breezes that those two environments created.

She had met the developer who helped her uncle build the house, and they had picked that spot for that very reason.

She drank a glass of freshly squeezed orange juice with a scoop of natural herbal Vitamin C powder to give it an even greater vitamin C oomph, then she plopped two elderberry vitamin gummies into her mouth and chewed them up as she did every day. They were tasty and gave her immune system a boost.

She brewed coffee and made breakfast. To Wally's delight, it was scrambled eggs with ham. She made a little plate for him.

"I spoil you rotten," she said as he meowed happily. He scarfed it up in about a millisecond and the kitty looked up at her and meowed, then he got on his two hind legs, plopping his two front paws on her leg.

"You're like Oliver Twist. Please, Sir, I Want Some More."

After breakfast, she put the dishes into the dishwasher and headed upstairs to shower. She called Ramón to make sure they were still on to go up to the reserve to get those orchids. He excitedly told her he was ready.

"Give me twenty minutes. I'll meet you out front," she said. She hung up and jumped into the shower.

She toweled off and applied sunscreen—a must living in the tropics, especially with her fair skin tone. She wore her brown hair short. Never in a million years did she ever think she would sport a pixie cut in her lifetime, but her long brown curls didn't mesh well living this close to the equator in a dusty, sandy beach town off the beaten path, so she went to a top stylist in the city and got herself her new coiffed hair. The stylist had asked her multiple times while brandishing the scissors in her face, "Are you sure you want to do this?"

Her mother and best friend Courtney almost had coronaries the first time they video-chatted with her new pixie cut, but they had grown to like her new look just as much as she did.

"You look beautiful with that Twiggy haircut," her mother had told her after she had gotten over the shock, Twiggy being the famous British model that rocked her iconic pixie haircut back in the sixties.

The other benefit of her short hairstyle was that she could quickly dry it, saving countless hours of coiffuring throughout the year.

She wore a long-sleeved V-neck white shirt that offered great sun protection and gray lightweight Capri pants that were perfect for outdoor working out, which she figured she had in store for her that morning helping Ramón and his cousin with the orchids.

She put on her wide-brimmed straw hat and headed downstairs as Wally curled up on the veranda off her master bedroom.

She opened the front door and Ramón and his cousin, Theo, were already there waiting. Since they were going to be doing gardening work, they had decided to use Ramón's pickup truck, much to Dana's chagrin, since she loved tooling around in her little Jeep Willys. Since it wasn't practical for this trip, Big Red would stay home.

"Good morning," Dana said cheerfully. Ramón and Theo smiled and greeted her warmly.

She had met Theo Villalobos several time, since he visited his cousin often and sometimes worked with him doing odd jobs on the property. He was also a master gardener who was the head groundkeeper at one of the fancy hotels near Sámara, which was fifteen miles from Mariposa Beach.

The cousins were only a year apart in age, with Ramón being the oldest. They were both only children, so they grew up close, more like brothers than first cousins.

Dana was looking over at the bed of the pickup truck, which was packed with tools and supplies.

"Boy, that's a lot of stuff you got there. This job must be bigger than I thought," Dana said. She figured it would be nice and easy to clip the orchids and bring them over to plant on her property, but knew next to nothing of gardening and even less about arboriculture.

"It's overkill, but that's Ramón's MO," Theo said teasingly.

"Better to have too many tools than not having the right ones you need and then we're scrambling around without them. Better to do this all in one visit before too many people are aware of what we're trying to accomplish," Ramón said.

"Makes sense," Dana said. She climbed into the front passenger seat. Theo climbed to the back of the pickup truck.

"Don't be silly, Theo, there's plenty of room in the front," Dana said, holding the door open for him. She gave her a shy smile and shook his head. "It's okay, more elbow room back here," he said.

"It's better anyway so we can make sure we don't lose any tools during the bumpy ride up the mountain," Ramón said.

Dana shrugged her shoulders, but she wasn't about to make a big deal about it if he felt more at ease riding along in the pickup truck bed versus squeezing in the front seat next to her.

Ramón fired up the truck and off they went. Ramón's wife, Carmen, came out to wave at them as they drove down her driveway and out towards Main Street, which would take them to the highway in the direction of the reserve.

Dana felt butterflies in her stomach, but she wasn't sure why. They not only had Doña Elsa's blessing but a signed legal document giving them permission to remove the orchids, but she felt like part of a burglary crew out on a heist.

# CHAPTER EIGHTEEN

BENNY WAS IN HIS OFFICE IN THE CITY. THE CLOSING HE had scheduled for ten a.m. had fallen apart. The buyers couldn't get the bank loan they said they could get, and now they wanted the seller to finance part of the deal. In other words, they didn't have the money to close the deal, thus killing it.

No matter how hard he worked to prevent these things from happening, they occurred enough that Benny had long ago learned to never count on collecting his closing fees until the actual money was sitting in his bank account.

He now had newfound time on his hands, so he decided to do a little digging on that Curt Bennett fellow. He was worried about Dana getting into the middle of this whole orchid thing. He didn't understand why she seemed to get into the middle of these sticky situations, but he knew she was just wired to try and help people who seemed to be up against the system on their own.

He figured it was baked into her San Francisco do-gooder DNA.

It was a fantastic quality, but it could and had put her in

danger, so he couldn't help but worry even though she would tell him to go fly a kite if he tried to talk her out of doing some of the things she did.

She was a strong-willed, headstrong woman; those were some of the traits that had made him fall in love with her. Her background as a former journalist made it hard for her to walk away from fights and doing her own investigation into things, much to the chagrin of the OIJ detectives like Jorge Picado.

But he still wanted to do his part in helping her, even if he was 150 miles away. He felt relieved that Doña Elsa had signed the legal document he had drafted which covered Dana's butt legally, but other dangerous issues could be lurking out there for her that couldn't be protected with a legal document.

The worst in people came out when there was big money at stake, and from Dana's preliminary investigation, there seemed to be a lot of money to be made off those orchids. And he agreed with Dana that it was way too much of a coincidence that Curt Bennett was in Mariposa Beach and near the wildflower reserve to then end up jailed trying to smuggle wildflowers out of the country.

So Benny began to look into the background of Curt Bennett. He paid a nice chunk of change every month to have access to some pretty impressive databases that were used in the legal community. Costa Rica didn't have such robust databases for its citizens—yet. Costa Ricans were also going down that road of giving up personal data to commercial companies that made a fortune off that data.

Since most of his clients were American expats, it was worth it for him to pay for that access, which came in handy when doing background checks. You could learn a lot about people with just a simple property tax search.

He began to tap away on his computer's keys while sipping on a cup of coffee.

"Lets see what I can find about you, Mr. Bennett," he said out loud to himself.

RAMÓN WAS A CAUTIOUS DRIVER, especially compared to Dana's spreading reputation for being lead-footed behind the wheel of Big Red. Toss in that he had his precarious tools and his cousin in the back of the pickup truck, he drove so slowly up to the reserve that Dana was convinced she could jump out and run up there faster on foot.

But she just smiled. She lived by the rule that whomever was behind the wheel made the driving rules, even if it meant the person was driving like one of the old biddies from the Gossip Brigade.

"So you sorted everything out with Claro?" Dana asked, trying to kill time.

"I did. He's excited we're coming and is waiting for us," Ramón said.

"Is Claro married?" Dana asked. Her curiosity was piqued.

"He's a widower," Ramón said, sounding sad.

"Oh, that poor man. He's not that old. His wife must have died young," Dana said.

"They were high school sweethearts. Married at eighteen. She died at thirty during the birth of their second child."

"Oh my gosh, how horrible."

Ramón nodded in glum agreement.

"And the child?" Dana was afraid to ask.

"She was born healthy and turned into a lovely young woman. Lives in San José with her husband and two children. She's Claro's pride and joy. His son too."

"Did he ever meet someone new?" Dana knew she was pushing Ramón's comfort level.

"Not that I'm aware. His love is that reserve. Just like Doña Elsa."

*Fair enough*, Dana thought as she looked out the window in silence, watching the countryside go by, reminding her about the beauty of the Costa Rican countryside. She thought about texting Max Perry to let him know she was going to be at the reserve, but he had ghosted for days now, so she figured she wouldn't impose herself on him. She figured he had a lot of his mind with his projects and his work at the reserve coming to an unexpected screeching halt months before it was supposed to end.

RAMÓN PULLED up to the front gate. Whereas it would usually be open for public tours in the morning, it had been locked up since the murder of Doña Elsa's husband and her arrest for that murder. A forbidding-looking black gate greeted them, but as soon as they pulled up, it began to open. On the other side was Claro Madderra waving them inside.

Ramón drove in, stopping to shake Claro's hand through the window.

Claro hunched down and peered into the window towards Dana.

"Good morning, Doña Dana," he said.

"Hello, Claro. It's a beautiful day."

"It sure is. Gets my mind off the uncertain times we're dealing with here in the reserve and with Doña Elsa."

Dana offered a tight, solemn smile, not knowing what else she could say or do.

"Need a ride?" Ramón asked with a smile. Dana was glad that he changed the subject.

It was a long drive up to the main building of the reserve. Dana had noticed that during their first visit. She thought Casa

Verde had a long driveway, but the reserve made it seem tiny in comparison.

"I'm good," he said, pointing at a black Yamaha utility ATV that was parked on the side of the driveway. He shook Theo's hand in the bed of the pickup truck then said to Ramón, "I'll meet you up there in front of the main building."

Ramón drove forward. Dana looked back as Claro closed the front gate and jumped on the ATV, quickly zipping by them and making them eat dust. A big smile was on his face as he waved at them from in front.

"Now those look like fun," Dana said.

"They are perfect for getting around here," Ramón said.

ATVs were a popular mode of transportation all across the coast. The locals used them to get around, and the tourists loved to rent them to go off-roading.

It was a big moneymaker for Big Mike's Surf Shop, and Dana had rented one from him a couple times. She was thinking it might be time to get one of her own. Maybe a red one to complement Big Red. *Small Red*, she thought with a smile.

Ramón parked in one of the visitor spots in front of the building that served as the reserve's main headquarters.

Claro had already parked the ATV and was waiting for them when Ramón parked. Theo climbed out of the pickup's truck bed. He stretched and dusted the road off his shirt the best he could.

Dana looked around. The last time she was at the reserve, it was bustling with activity, with dozens of young interns and staff plus visitors getting ready to tour the wildflower reserve. Now she could only see one other staff member. She could tell who he was because he wore a red polo shirt with the reserve's logo of wild orchids embroidered on the shirt's left chest and the word STAFF emblazoned in yellow on the back of the shirt.

"Where is everyone?" she asked.

"Gone," Claro said, looking around sadly. "With parents and students freaking about having a murder on the property, the schools shut down the programs almost immediately; within days just a handful stayed against their parents' wishes. But now only two remain even though they're not getting credit for their schoolwork and the payments have stopped. We have enough food to feed them and our staff for another ten days, then that's it. We'll have to send everyone home."

"How terrible," Dana said.

"Doña Elsa was the heart and soul to the reserve. We never planned or discussed how we could continue to operate the reserve without her, so we're in a bad spot. That's why I'm glad you're here to save those orchids, because this will probably end up becoming a resort or high-priced condos for rich expats if Gustavo Barca has his way."

"I doubt he would care about the wildflowers," Dana said.

"Wildflowers like those rare orchids take a lot of work and love; they're not really suitable for the landscaping that Gustavo Barca puts in, which are palm trees, cacti, and bamboo plants. Easy and cheap to maintain. And of course we have the pharma reps hanging around like vultures to see what they can pick off the soon-to-be carcass of the reserve."

"I'm so sorry for everything that is happening," Dana said.

"It is what it is. I'm more worried about Doña Elsa getting locked up for a murder she didn't commit," Claro said.

"So who do you think killer her husband?"

"He was a scheming shyster. The list of suspects would be huge, but I can't get the police to even bother to look at anyone else. They have focused on Doña Elsa and that's it. They have blinders on."

Dana could hear and feel the frustration coming from him. She wanted to trust that the legal system would work and if

Doña Elsa was really innocent, then she would soon be set free, but it didn't always work out that way.

Just then she saw Iris Kjellberg walking out from the dorm area. Dana remembered the pretty student from Sweden. She was surprised she was still at the reserve.

"Hi, Iris," Dana said.

The young girl seemed a bit standoffish, especially since she had been so friendly the first time they had met.

"Hello," she said, ice-cold.

*Um, okay*, Dana thought.

"Is your friend Lydia still here?" Dana asked.

"She wasn't really my friend, just my bunkmate, and no, she deserted the reserve. Hightailed it back to Germany, running back to Mommy and Daddy."

*Well, this conversation has turned awkward.*

"Well, with the schools terminating the programs, it makes sense. Don't your parents want you back home? A man was murdered, after all," Dana said.

"And his killer, Elsa Calderón, is in jail where she belongs. No need for the knee-jerk reaction of all the schools and for these students who were supposedly here for the reserve to run off at the first hardship," Iris said.

That took Dana aback.

"Doña Elsa hasn't even been charged with anything yet. She's under preventive detention, so it's a bit premature to assume she's guilty," Ramón said, sounding upset.

Iris responded with a millennial eye roll. Dana could all but hear her thinking *okay, boomer.*

"Is Max Perry around?" Dana asked, hoping to change the subject.

"No. So what are you doing here, anyway?" Iris said.

Dana told her.

"Wait, you can't do that without Max's permission," Iris huffed.

"Um, no, we just need Doña Elsa's permission. Which we have. In writing," Dana said.

"I'm calling Max," Iris said as she stormed off into the headquarters building.

Dana stood there, stunned. She turned to Claro. "What. Was. That about?"

He shrugged it off. "Well, I didn't want to say anything since he's your friend, but he's been very difficult since Doña Elsa was arrested. He thinks he's in charge. And he's a bit tyrannical about it and can't stand that I'm really the one in charge in her absence."

"Really? Why?"

Claro shrugged his shoulders again. "I guess he thinks I'm just an uneducated peon and he has all these fancy college degrees and is getting his Ph.D., so he doesn't feel the need to listen to me about anything. He keeps telling me he's the one who knows what's best for those orchids, not me. He chewed me out about letting Ramón come here to take those orchids. He threatened to call the police and have us arrested for theft."

"Really?" Dana couldn't believe it. He seemed so kind just a few days ago.

"Well, we have Doña Elsa's permission and Doña Dana has a signed document notarized by Don Benny, who's a lawyer, so it's all nice and legal. So don't you worry, Claro. We're taking those orchids to Casa Verde," Ramón said.

"Good, because the way he was talking, we might need it. So we better get to work before he shows up," Claro said.

"Let's do it," Dana said, pulling on the chin drawstring from her straw hat to make it get even snugger to her scalp, which caused Ramón, Claro, and Theo to start laughing.

She felt a little embarrassed but was happy to alleviate what was turning out to be a stressful situation. And it was about to get worse.

# CHAPTER NINETEEN

DANA THOUGHT THE PROCESS OF GETTING TO THE ORCHIDS would be easy, like buying a flower from a greenhouse to bring home to plant. She was wrong.

First of all, she didn't realize how big the reserve was: over five thousand acres, according to Claro Madderra. The drive down reminded Dana of Mad Max Fury Road. Ramón was driving in his pickup with Theo in the passenger side and flanked by Claro and Dana on ATVs. Dana was having a blast maneuvering the quad off-road and thinking *I really need to get one of these.*

These were not the same orchids she saw the last time she was here. It took them an hour through rough terrain to drive from the reserve's main building down to the area where the rare orchids grew. It was an area off-limits to visitors.

The drive over was awe-inspiring. It was an absolute gem of Costa Rican wildflowers, and although the timing for going there was horrible—Don Eladio was dead, Doña Elsa in jail, the reserve's future doubtful—from a wildflower perspective, the timing weather-wise was perfect. Something that Claro and Ramón had warned her about was to ensure that she didn't miss out, since she was about to witness some of the province's most abundant and diverse wildflower blooms. And although the entire reserve is thousands of acres, the section where the rare orchids and the other flowers bloom was on a hundred-acre section.

Dana drove the ATV through the green, lush, rolling hills following Claro, since Ramón was still driving slow well behind them. She drove down an embankment and Claro stopped, so she did the same. She pulled beside him as he got off the ATV. He was looking down the embankment, so she did the same and was in awe. It was like a spiritual experience, what she felt, looking at thousands upon thousands of wildflowers. A cornucopia of vivid colors overwhelmed her neurological system. Pink, gold, bright oranges, purple, red, white. Beautiful flowers spread everywhere like weeds. She noticed some tulips, and the surrounding areas were lavender fields in full bloom that reminded Dana of the French countryside. She had no idea lavender could grow like this in the tropics. Most everything was unknown to her, since that was the extent of her flower knowledge.

"Oh my gosh," was all she could say for a while, then finally she could speak again. "What kind of flowers are those?"

Claro smiled wide. "It would take a while to answer that question," he said, smiling even wider.

Dana looked at him, puzzled.

"You see, there are at least four hundred different species of plants and flowers down there."

"Oh my goodness. That's unbelievable."

Just then Ramón pulled up in his pickup with Theo. Dana saw he exited the truck smiling, so she figured he knew what was going on.

"Spectacular, isn't it?" Ramón said.

The four of them stood there for about a minute, Dana snapping a few photographs from her iPhone.

"I truly hope Gustavo doesn't end up building a condo tower down there," Dana said wistfully.

"Let's hope not," Claro said.

The thought that that could even be a possibility was stirring anger inside of Dana. There was something she could do. Could. *No, should,* she said to herself, looking down that breathtaking valley of flowers.

"There is no way we could take samplings of more than just the orchids," Dana wondered out loud.

"Not just the four of us. It would be too much to handle," Claro said.

"The orchids are the rarest of the flowers here. Especially the kind that we'll find down there that you can't find anywhere else in the country, so we need to save them first, and then we can think about what else we can do about the other flowers," Ramón said.

Made sense to Dana. They were here for the orchids right now, so they needed to focus on that.

Everyone hopped back on their vehicles as they made their way down towards the location of the orchids. It took longer than expected since they had to drive around the beautiful field of blooming flowers. After about ten minutes Claro parked his ATV and hopped off. Dana followed suit.

"Where are they?" she said, looking around.

"About a ten-minute walk that way," Claro said, pointing towards a small creek.

A couple minutes later, Ramón arrived and parked. He and Theo climbed out and got the tools needed from the pickup truck's bed and they walked down towards the creek.

It was warm, but there was a cooling mist in the air. The sounds of critters scurrying around mixed in with crickets, frogs croaking, the wind rustling through the lavender and grass fields, and birds chirping. It sounded like Brain FM's nature sounds, but live and without the monthly subscription.

After about ten minutes, they arrived at their destination.

"There they are," Ramón said in awe.

*Hmmm*, Dana thought. They didn't look as spectacular as she thought they were going to look after all the talk about them and after witnessing all the other blooming beauties that were all around them. Maybe she was getting jaded after seeing so much beauty. She looked at them again, and they did have a regal beauty to them. They were bright white, with five or six leaves each. They had a modest beauty about them in comparison to the vibrantly colored flowers she had seen before. They gave off an air of pristine beauty that made it easier to appreciate the form of the flower rather than being overwhelmed by color.

"So you're the ones everyone is talking about," Dana said to the orchids. She knelt down to get a close look. They emanated a captivating fragrance that caught Dana by surprise.

"Wow, they smell amazing," she said, closing her eyes and taking a deep breath. She felt her body tingling from the smells.

Claro bent down and plucked off one of the leaves and gave it to Dana. She looked at it in the palm of her hand.

"They look like one of the pastry petals from my wedding cake."

Claro said, "Like those on the cake, these are edible too." He smiled as he tore off a tiny piece of the petal and put it in his mouth. Ramón and Theo did the same. Claro offered a tiny piece to her. Dana took it with curiosity. "What does it taste like?"

Claro, Ramón, and Theo smiled wide-eyed. "It's a bit intoxicating, like a drug. Your mouth will tingle and your lips will feel numb," Claro said.

"Really? From just this little bitty piece of the flower?" Dana said, holding it in the air for closer inspection. She was skeptical.

The men nodded.

"How long does that feeling last?"

"Just a couple minutes," Claro said.

Dana shrugged her shoulders. "When in Rome," she said, plopping the tiny chunk of flower into her mouth.

It tasted tart. Like Sour Patch candy. She puckered her lips and her eyes watered a little as Claro, Ramón, and Theo laughed.

It was an odd feeling. And a few seconds later she felt the numbness in her mouth, which freaked her out for a moment. She didn't have much time to worry about it, since the feeling dissipated as fast as it had started. Within a minute she had feeling back in her mouth, but her body still felt a little bit tingly.

"You weren't kidding. That was wild," Dana said to Claro.

"Some more?" he said, offering a big piece of the flower.

"No thanks, that's it for me. I know I'm a prude," she said, smiling.

"Okay, let's get to work. Time is of the essence," Ramón said.

They laid out the gardening tools they had brought along. They put on gloves and got to work.

Little did Dana know how accurate Ramón's statement was —time was of the essence. And it was about to run out on them.

# CHAPTER TWENTY

It took over an hour of tolling in the field before they had what they came for—enough of these snow-white-colored orchids to transplant onto Dana's property.

Claro and Ramón were the expert gardeners, so they did the delicate work of picking the orchids and taking the flowers they felt had the best chance of surviving at Casa Verde.

Theo and Dana did the grunt work: handing and removing tools like a nurse aiding a surgeon and preparing the containers where the orchids would be stored for the drive back to Mariposa Beach. Dana was in awe of seeing the two master gardeners at work.

Claro carefully handled the storage bins for the orchids as if he were handling iron rods in a nuclear plant. Once everything was gently and carefully packed in Ramón's pickup, he smiled.

"We did it," Claro said, holding his hand up in the air for high-fives.

Dana had a Seinfeld-like disdain for the high five, but wasn't a barbarian who would leave him hanging, so she high-fived back and then had to exchange high-fives with Ramón and Theo, who wanted in on the high five action.

Dana acquiesced silently with a grin. Once everyone had exchanged celebratory high fives, they got back to their vehicles and made the drive back to the reserve's headquarters.

Dana and Claro arrived first in the ATV, and she was taken aback by the homecoming greeting that awaited them.

She saw a white police sedan with two uniformed officers leaning up against it. Parked next to it was an unmarked white Toyota Corolla she knew belonged to Jorge Picado, the Judicial Police detective who was the bane of Dana's Guanacaste Province existence.

It seemed that they had been waiting for them to return from the field.

"What's going on?" Dana said, removing the black helmet.

Claro drove without a helmet and even teased Dana's request for one. "Safety first," she had replied. *You can be macho dumb-dumb, but not me,* she had thought.

She didn't see Detective Picado but saw Detective Gabriela Rojas walking towards her.

"Hi, Gabriela. What's going on?"

She looked sheepish.

"Well... we got a call..." she began to say before being interrupted by Max Perry, who came out of the headquarters building like a bat out of hell.

"There they are," Perry said.

Detective Picado exited the building behind Perry.

The mustached detective eyed her down as usual.

"Every time a crime occurs... there you are," he said, sounding annoyed.

"Crime? What crime?" Dana asked.

"I would like to know as well what crime has been supposedly committed here?" Claro said.

"Stealing protected wildflowers," Perry said, which caused Picado to give him a *shut your mouth* look. He did just that.

"What are you talking about, Max?" Dana said, getting angry.

"You address me, not him," Picado snapped.

"Fine, what are *you* talking about?" she snapped back.

"Mr. Perry called the police about the removal of protected flowers, and since this is also still my crime scene, I figured I better see what shenanigans you're up to again," Picado said.

"Oh brother, we're not up to any darn shenanigans, Detective."

"What is that, then?" Iris said, pointing to the back of Ramón's pickup truck.

Picado and Rojas walked over with Perry following right behind.

Scores of the white orchids lay carefully in the cardboard boxes Ramón had brought along to transport them back to Casa Verde.

"We have permission. From the owner of this property and everything on it," Dana said, producing a copy of the signed legal document.

It took fifteen minutes of wrangling back and forth between Perry, Iris, the detectives, and Dana, Ramón, and Claro about whether or not they could legally remove those orchids from the reserve. Theo sat out during the back-and-forth, seemingly wanting to be anywhere but there at that time. The few remaining staff members had also gathered around the sidelines to witness the show.

When Picado had heard enough, he told everyone to stay put while he and Rojas discussed the situation.

"What is going on with you, Max?" Dana asked, feeling shocked about his behavior.

"I'm sorry, but those orchids are too valuable to the ecology of this region to let folks who don't know what they're doing make a mess of the ecosystem," he lectured.

"What are you talking about? We didn't remove all the orchids, just a few to ensure they survive once Gustavo Barca buys all this land and bulldozes over that land to put up his tower of luxury condos for the bon vivant," Dana said.

"You don't understand about these issues. I have a Ph.D.," he said dismissively.

She was about to tell him to go fly a kite when Picado interrupted them.

"This is a reserve, yes, but it's not a public one. It's on private land owned by Elsa Calderón. We telephoned the police station where she's being held and she confirms that the legal document is correct and that these people have her permission to take whatever they want from her property," Picado said, waving his hand towards Dana's corner. Dana was surprised. It was the first time Picado had even hinted about her being on the right end of a legal dispute.

"That is preposterous," Perry said.

"That is the law. If you have any issues with what's going on, then take it up in the civil courts. We're done here," Picado said, turning away and walking towards his car.

Rojas winked at Dana and smiled as she followed Picado back to the car. They got into the car and drove away.

Perry was still protesting about the travesty of it all, the irresponsibility, and how he was going to sue. Dana and the others ignored him as they prepared to leave. Feeling the cold shoulder from everyone but Iris, Perry shouted, "Forget you all," and he stormed off like a child storming off a playground, upset over perceived slights that were all in his head.

Iris flipped Dana the bird. That shocked her so badly that she just began to laugh at the absurdity of it all. Iris then turned away and ran off after Perry.

"Young people like that make we weep for our future sometimes," Ramón said.

"She sure seems very chummy with Max. Wonder if she's hot for teacher," Dana said.

"Well, I can only say what I've perceived with my own two eyes, but Mr. Perry seemed to get very friendly with several of the young female students in the months he was here. They seemed to have gotten very close, if you get what I mean," Claro said.

"Wow. And here I thought life at a wildflower reserve was studious and boring," Dana said.

"I could write a book," Claro said with a devilish grin.

"So what are you going to do about Max?"

"I'm going to let him know he's longer welcome to stay here. I'll give him until the morning to pack his bag and leave. But don't worry about all that. You and Ramón get back to Casa Verde and make sure those orchids are protected. I don't trust those two," Claro said, looking towards the student dorms were Perry and Iris had disappeared.

Dana, Ramón, and Theo left the reserve, heading back to Mariposa Beach. Her gut was telling her that this wasn't the last she would see of Max Perry, and she figured he would be even more upset once Claro kicked him out. The thought sent shivers down her spine. Seeing him in that new ugly light she saw him in just then made her wonder what else he could be capable of. The fact was she didn't know him from Adam. She had known him for just a few days and had only interacted with him a couple times face-to-face, so why was she so shocked about his boorish behavior? And why was he so adamant in preventing her from taking those orchids? What was the real reason for that fury and to call the police? And what else could he have been capable of doing to be in control of those orchids? Those were the types of questions she kept asking herself as they drove back to Casa Verde in near silence the whole way.

# CHAPTER TWENTY-ONE

DANA ARRIVED AT THE CAFE SLASH BOOKSTORE IN TIME FOR closing.

"How did it go at the reserve?" Mindy asked.

Dana blew air out of her cheeks and rolled her eyes.

"That well, huh?" Mindy said while laughing out loud.

There were a couple customers waiting for their lattes, and one of the expat locals, Bill Kingman, who owned a catamaran to take tourists out deep-sea fishing, was perusing the book-shelves, so she didn't want to get into the details in front of customers.

"I'll give the lowdown during closing," Dana said, walking into the book side of the bookstore slash cafe.

Amalfi was manning the register.

"How's today been?" Dana asked.

"A bit on the slow side. The e-reader rentals were hopping, though."

"Little earners, those electric buggers," Dana said with a smile. "I'll be in the office."

On the way to the back where her office was located, she

chatted with Kingman, who was perusing the mystery/thriller section of her backlist paperbacks. He was one of her best customers. "Hey, Dave, the new Jack Reacher is coming out in November. It's called *The Midnight Line,* and I should have copies coming by December," Dana said.

Kingman lit up in excitement. "Awesome, make sure to hold a copy for me, please."

"Of course, like always," Dana said.

She headed back to her office to begin prepping for the end-of-day wrap-up. She checked her Point-of-Sale system, and it was a decent day with the e-reader rentals once again saving the day. As usual, the e-readers preloaded with romance and thriller ebooks were the most popular. She questioned why she should bother to continue offering the literary packet. People came to the sun and fun of the tropics to relax and get away from the real world, and their reading tastes reflected that they just wanted a fun beach read, nothing too heavy. Real life was heavy enough.

She glanced over at her computer monitor that displayed her indoor and outdoor security cameras all displayed in gallery view like she was watching Hollywood Squares. Amalfi was ringing up Dave Kingman. A tourist was sipping on a latte while reading a book on one of the comfy love chairs she had put out. She glanced at the camera looking outside right in front of her shop and saw Max Perry heading inside. *Oh great*, she thought.

Dana was expecting a confrontation, but Perry was contrite.

"This morning... well, things escalated quickly," Perry said.

Dana nodded in agreement.

"I just wanted to apologize and let you know that what happened at the reserve wasn't directed at you or anyone else, it's just that Claro and I had been butting heads since I set foot on the reserve. He was jealous about how close Doña Elsa and I had become, and she trusted me one hundred percent, and since I'm a scientist, she wanted me to be the arborist and botanist for the reserve. That way she could focus on being the face of the reserve to bring in donations, tourists, and students. That threatened Claro, who had filled in that role for years. But he's an amateur. Don't get me wrong, he's a fine gardener, but not a professional and trained botanist and arborist like me. So he made it his mission to try and cut me down. It's been tense between us for months, and we both tried to bottle it in for Doña Elsa's sake, but now that she's gone, all that tension and resentment bottled out like a well-shaken soda can. And that's what you witnessed this morning. And I'm embarrassed."

Yikes. Dana didn't know what to say to all that. She took a moment to process it all in her head.

"That's fine. And I don't want to get in the middle of you two or any dealings going on at the reserve; that's not my business. I was just helping out Ramón, who is my friend, and to whom Doña Elsa has trusted to care for her orchids, and that's it. Everything else is between you and Claro," Dana said.

Perry held his hands in the air in surrender. "I understand, and I don't blame you. I know it's messy. And I shouldn't have overacted. So Ramón is just going to plant those orchids in your land?"

"That's right."

"So Claro isn't involved in that project?"

"No, it's just Ramón. I suppose I'll help him along with his wife, Carmen."

"And these will only be planted on your property?"

Dana looked at him suspiciously.

"Sorry for the twenty questions, but I just want what's best for those orchids to ensure their survival. That's it, Scout's honor," Perry said with a smile as he held his fingers in the Boy Scouts sign.

"Look, Max, I like Claro. No, he isn't involved, but he's welcome to visit my property to see the orchids once they're planted," Dana said.

"Of course. I just want to make sure he's not going to mess that up."

"Ramón is the one handling the orchids now, not Claro."

"And they're just on your property, right? I ask because there are pharmaceutical reps hanging around town who would love to get their hands on those orchids, and Doña Elsa was adamant that for-profit cosmetic-type pharma companies had to keep their hands off those plants."

"I'm aware of Doña Elsa's wishes and will be honoring them," Dana said.

"Okay, great. That's what I wanted to hear. I'll get out of your hair then. No more problems from me, okay?" Perry said.

"Okay," Dana said.

With that out of the way, Perry said goodbye and began to make his way outside. He had the door opened when something struck Dana's curiosity.

"Say, Max," she called out to him before he left.

He stopped and turned to face her as he held the door open.

"What's up?"

"I thought you were leaving soon. Why are you getting all wrapped up in this situation?"

He smiled. "I love it here. And I think I can do a lot of good here. So I'm staying. I'd like to take over the reserve for Doña Elsa. Run things for her until she gets back."

"So what will happen to Claro?"

"Well, he kicked me out. Until I can get control of the reserve, there isn't much I can do. But I'll fight him in court."

"So you're not going back to Hawaii?"

"There is still important work I need to do here," Perry said.

He said goodbye and left.

"What was all that about?" Mindy asked after he was gone.

"I don't know, but I have a feeling things are going to get even wilder at the wild reserve," Dana said, sounding ominous.

# CHAPTER TWENTY-TWO

THAT NIGHT DANA HAD A LOVELY DINNER PLANNED BY herself. She had been an introvert her whole life, preferring quiet evenings at home with a good book or TV show. Life as a journalist and later as a public relations person was tough on her psyche, having to be out there front and center dealing with people. So she savored these moments, or was that just her brain triggering those thoughts to hold the other thoughts that she was in her mid-thirties and her boyfriend lived over one hundred and fifty miles away.

*Meow.*

Dana looked down at Wally and smiled. "You're right, I'm not alone, I have you," she said, and laughed out loud. Wally was prancing at her feet.

"You just want my tuna, don't you?"

One of the perks of having a deep-sea fisherman like Dave Kingman as an avid thriller reader and her best customer was that he always held a few steaks for her when he got back in town. He usually came back to town with marlin, sailfish, Dorado—mahi mahi—or yellowfin tuna, what he had caught on his latest trip and Dana's favorite.

She had left one of her five tuna steaks thawing in the refrigerator all day and now it was ready to eat. She chopped up some garlic and tossed it into a frying pan lightly oiled with olive oil. She let the garlic sizzle for a minute and added the tuna steak to it. After three minutes she flipped the steak over and let it cook for another three minutes. Perfect.

She had made some sushi rice in her Instant Pot. She scooped up some of the rice onto a plate. Next she cooked some chopped-up kale for a few minutes in olive oil and added that to the plate. She plopped the tuna steak onto the kale. She took a step back and admired her plating. She poured a glass of chilled Sauvignon Blanc and presto, dinnertime.

After the weird day she had, she was in the mood for some creepy classical music, so she asked Alexa to play some Verdi. He didn't disappoint.

Dana was tidying up the kitchen when Benny called. He would be coming down to Mariposa Beach the next day for the weekend, and she couldn't wait to see him.

She told him about the brouhaha at the reserve between Max Perry and Claro Madderra.

"Never a dull moment down there," Benny said.

Then she told him about Max Perry visiting her at the bookstore that afternoon and his plans of taking over the reserve.

"Well, good luck with that. Doña Elsa has had suitors for that land for the better part of two decades now, and she's not interested in selling. I guess with everything going down, she might be more open to that now, but Max would need some deep pockets to buy all those acres.

"So when is Ramón going to plant those orchids in your land?" Benny asked.

"He wants to get everything perfect, but he said that by tomorrow or Saturday morning at the latest."

"It's going to be wild if those orchids take off and grow in Casa Verde," Benny said.

"Ramón seems confident they will, and Claro agreed. Of course, Max said it's a crazy notion to think they would take. I guess we'll know soon enough.

"How was your day?" Dana asked.

"I had a closing fall apart, so that always stinks."

"Oh, I'm sorry about that, hon."

"It's okay, it comes with the territory. It also freed some time on my schedule, so I did some snooping myself."

Dana was intrigued.

"Oh, sounds exciting."

"Hardy har-har, mister. So let's have it. Whatcha got for me?"

"I did some digging into Curt Bennett and his arrest."

Now that almost made Dana fall off her chair. Benny seemed to always be against that type of stuff unless it was work related.

"My, my, my, what a snoop," Dana mocked.

"What can I say? Your curiosity about everything must be rubbing off on me," Benny said.

Benny told Dana about Curt Bennett's background in the pharmaceutical trade, which jived with what Dana had deduced from finding his LinkedIn page.

"He was under contract by Forever Young Corporation. That is why he was in the country on some sort of business trip for them."

"Forever Young, skin care company," Dana said. "You know, Doña Elsa said there was a pharma company that wanted to buy her orchids. They held their cards close to the chest, but the story around the campfire is they're developing a Botox cream that would generate the same results as injecting yourself. That stuff would be worth millions."

"A cream over a needle to the face, I can see the appeal," Benny said.

"That can't be a coincidence," Dana said.

"Seems unlikely to me as well. Especially since I have it on good authority that he was indeed busted with smuggling out orchids among other plants."

"What? Wow. That's huge, Benny. He must have gotten those from the reserve somehow."

"We don't know that. Maybe after getting shot down by Doña Elsa, he was able to source those orchids from somewhere else in the country. I understand they're rare, but I find it hard to believe the only place they could be found is at the reserve," Benny said.

"I'm not an expert, but it seems they grow in the wild there and nowhere else nearby, at least that has been discovered.

"Okay, so Doña Elsa turns him away then she ends up killing her husband, giving him a huge opportunity to pounce with her sitting in jail," Benny said.

"I don't know, Benny. I'm starting to think she didn't kill her husband. Besides, Curt Bennett was already leaving the country with the orchids, so he had already accomplished getting his hands on them, and that was before Doña Elsa's husband was killed and she was locked up."

"So either he got the flowers from the reserve there or he found them somewhere else."

"Doubtful. And if he did get his hands on those orchids from the reserve, he would need inside help to do that," Dana said.

She sighed.

"What are you thinking?" Benny asked

"That someone inside the reserve must have betrayed Doña Elsa. Someone close to her."

# CHAPTER TWENTY-THREE

DANA TOSSED AND TURNED ALL NIGHT, MUCH TO THE annoyance of her cat, who had to move around the bed as she rolled over from one side to the other, trying to find the sweet spot to fall asleep.

She couldn't help it. All she could think about were the orchids, Doña Elsa and her dead husband, and that someone must have stabbed her in the back.

Still a better fate than her husband went through, being that he was actually stabbed with shears in the chest.

"It's pointless," she said out loud as she kicked off her bed sheet and got out of bed. There was a full moon and it was a cool night, a welcome change, so she had the shades drawn open and the sliding door that led from her master bedroom to her veranda was slid open to let the nice breeze from the Pacific cool things down.

The full moon was so bright that she didn't even need to turn her lights on. She just walked outside to her veranda and leaned over its railing, taking the beauty of her surroundings. *It's a shame humans are better wired to function during the daytime, because the night is so serene, calm, and beautiful.* Dana closed her eyes and took a deep breath. She thought about her options. Meditation or watch something silly on Netflix. Zombieing out in front of the television made her sleepy. She opened her eyes and saw something from the corner of her eye that got her attention.

*Is that a light?* she thought. For a moment her mind convinced her she was looking at fireflies before the reality set in. *That's a flashlight.*

She watched the light bouncing around down below near her greenhouse in utter confusion. Her mind was asking and answering questions. *A flashlight? Yes, a flashlight. Is that Ramón out there? At this hour, no way. Okay, so what now? I don't know.*

She was about to yell down there but then stopped herself. For all she knew, they were armed burglars down there. And she was here alone. She ducked down low, but since it was dark out, she would be hard to spot from that distance, so she felt a bit safe about that.

She had to call the police, but they would be twenty minutes away, if she was lucky. A drawback of living off the beaten path.

She went back inside. Wally was snoring in her bed. "Some protector you are," she whispered. She went into her closet and grabbed her uncle's .22 rifle. She kept it loaded. She looked outside again and could see the flashlight bouncing around in the same area. The intruder didn't seem to be headed towards the house. They seemed to be focusing on the greenhouse. A good thing, since they were not breaking into her home, but bizarre that they seemed to be hanging around the greenhouse. Maybe they were lost or formulating a plan of attack in order to break into her house.

She grabbed her cell phone and called Ramón. His house was about one hundred yards away versus the closest police substation that was ten miles away. The phone rang five times before a very groggy Ramón answered the phone.

"Doña Dana, are you all right?"

She told him about the intruders.

"I'll be right there," he said, hanging up.

Dana felt relieved she had Ramón and Carmen living nearby. She grabbed the rifle and made her way back to the veranda. She saw Ramón running towards the greenhouse with his own flashlight and his machete in hand.

"Hey, you," he yelled loudly.

Dana decided it was time to let them know they were busted, so she turned on the lights to her bedroom and the veranda, which shone down towards the greenhouse.

If the intruders thought they were still undetected, they now knew otherwise and oh, how the tables had turned.

"I'm armed," Dana said loudly. She fired one time up in the air to make her point.

She couldn't see the intruder but saw that the flashlight was moving fast, flickering all over the place as it began to head away from the greenhouse and away from Ramón, who was yelling at them to leave.

They obliged. She heard frantic running, and near the wall of the property the flashlight went dark. Dana figured they didn't want them to see their whereabouts as they probably jumped over the wall and scurried away like a roach trying to escape when you turn on the lights to a darkened room.

"I'm calling the police," Dana shouted, then she shouted at Ramón, "be careful, Ramón."

"Ramón, don't chase them," his wife shouted out towards him as well.

Dana turned to see her standing there in her nightgown.

"Did you call the police?" Dana asked Carmen.

"Yes, they're on the way, but it will be a while," she said, sounding and looking nervous for her husband's safety.

Dana made her way downstairs, noticing that Wally was long gone from her bed. With all the commotion and the sound of gunfire, he would be hiding for a day or two.

In the entryway of the house, Dana turned on all the outdoor lights as she went outside.

She held onto the rifle and joined Carmen, who was still standing there by the driveway. A look of terror on her face quickly dissipated into a weary smile when she saw Ramón walking back towards them with his flashlight and machete.

He smiled and hugged his wife.

"They're gone," he said.

"Are you sure?" Dana asked.

"Oh yes, I saw a shadow clear the wall. Pretty impressive," he said.

"How many were they?"

"I think it was one person. But after they cleared the wall, I heard what sounded like that person getting into a car and then the car took off. Fast."

"This is so scary," Dana said. Then she started feeling angry at the violation.

At home is where people feel the safest, and to have that sanctuary violated this way was unsettling.

🦇

TWENTY-SEVEN MINUTES LATER, the police arrived.

"Good thing they ran off, with this slow-as-molasses response," Dana said.

They opened the front gate and Officer Freddy Sánchez drove up in his official police motocross bike.

He took their statement and went to look around the

perimeter, something Ramón and Dana had already done. Dana pointed out to a piece of fabric clothing that was left dangling in the barbed wire that lined the top of the wall. The intruder had also left behind what looked like a thick blanket that they had draped over the barbed wire and jagged pieces of broken glass that served as a theft deterrent. Dana looked at the items left behind by the intruder, who had left in such a hurry that they left those juicy clues behind for the police.

Sánchez looked up and pointed at the item draped over the wall and the piece of fabric dangling from the barbed wire. He smiled.

"We don't usually get this lucky," he said. "Can I borrow a ladder?"

# CHAPTER TWENTY-FOUR

Iris Kjellberg might have as well left her ID and a detailed itinerary behind at Dana's Casa Verde. The thick military-style green blanket she used to drape over the barbed wall at Dana's was stamped with Doña Elsa's reserve's name and logo.

It took Detective Picado about a millisecond to find the reserve's student dorms stocked jam-full with the exact same type of blankets in a linen closet.

Rosita Vezzoso, who was in charge of housekeeping for the reserve, confirmed that was one of their blankets. She even checked her inventory in stock, and they were missing one blanket.

The piece of fabric found snagged on the barbed wire fit the polo shirt issued to the interns down to a T.

There was also the wad of human hair left behind on that pesky barbed wire. It was blonde. Same hair color as Iris, whose bright Swedish goldilocks stood out in the tropics.

And the cherry on top for the police was the white cloth gauze Iris had wrapped around her right hand. Upon inspection, police could determine that the wound appeared to be from a nasty cut on something very sharp. And a wound the police were familiar with when burglars injured themselves trying to maneuver over the ubiquitous barbed wire that is used in just about every private and commercial property in the country.

It didn't take long for her to break down in tears and admit to being the person who broke into Dana's property.

"But why?" Dana asked Detective Rojas.

"She claims she wanted to rescue the orchids you stole from the reserve," Rojas said.

"Oh, brother."

"I know. But in her mind that's what she was doing."

"You'll need to file a report at the OIJ substation in Nicoya," Detective Picado interrupted.

Dana looked at Benny, who had arrived in town that afternoon.

"Can I talk to her?" Dana asked.

Rojas and Picado looked at each other and shrugged their shoulders.

"I'm done here. Like I said, if you want to move forward with this case, you'll need to drive up to Nicoya and file a report on Monday," Picado said as he walked back to his car.

"She's being held at the holding cell in Nicoya," Rojas said.

"The same one where Doña Elsa is being held?" Dana asked.

"That's the one. It's a small jail, since it's only meant to hold someone for a few days, so they're probably in the same holding cell," Rojas said.

"Oh, the irony," Dana said, mostly to herself.

Rojas nodded in agreement. "I don't know what's going on, but looks like the whole reserve has been cursed because of those darn white orchids. I would get rid of those, Dana. I wouldn't want those anywhere near my house," Rojas said as she gave herself the sign of the cross.

The horn blared. It was Picado hurrying his partner up. Rojas rolled her eyes. "Gotta go. Get rid of those flowers. Bad juju," she said again as she left.

"Do you believe in bad juju?" Dana asked Benny with a grin.

"That would be a no." She knew that would be his answer, since he was one of the most practical, fact-based thinkers she had ever met.

Dana believed in karma and all that, but not that those orchids could be cursed. The reason those flowers were the cause for all the shenanigans that had gone on the past week was greed. And she was resolved to get to the bottom of it once and for all. And to do that she needed to talk to Iris to find out just what the heck she was thinking, breaking into her home.

ON MONDAY, Dana and Benny made the drive up to Nicoya. They had to go there anyway to file a crime report, and she hoped to talk to that little Swedish scoundrel.

"Second trip in three days to visit yet another person I know behind bars," Dana said. She was half joking about it because it was too surreal to deal with the reality of it all.

"I tell you what," she contained saying, "this better be the last time in a long while."

"I'm not sure what you're hoping to accomplish driving up here. I don't think Iris is going to be willing to help you out. Especially since the police believe she acted on her own, breaking in to steal those orchids," Benny said as he drove.

"I think she's being used."

"By whom?"

"I'm not sure, but it seems that Max Perry and Claro Madderra are both after the reserve, so perhaps one of them is behind this whole mess."

Benny nodded in agreement. "Land is what's valuable, and Doña Elsa has a lot of it."

"You don't think this is about those orchids?" Dana asked.

"Not anymore."

"Perhaps. But one thing is for sure," Dana said, looking out the window at the countryside blurring by, "whoever controls the reserve has control over the orchids. Especially if they get rid of the ones I have."

Benny drove his Toyota Land Cruiser into town and parked in front of the police station. They stepped out from the air-conditioned vehicle and were greeted by the heat and stickiness of Nicoya. The temperature was in the low nineties, but the mugginess made it feel even warmer. Once inside the station, the same receptionist that had helped Dana and Ramón out greeted them. She scrunched up her face as if she was trying to place Dana.

"May I help you?"

They went through the same ordeal as before and then were ushered into the waiting area. Dana sat on the same orange plastic chair and waited. About ten minutes later, a uniformed police officer showed up. He was much friendlier than the one from the other day. He cheerfully went over the visiting rules then ushered them into the visiting room before walking away, whistling a song that sounded very familiar to Dana, but she couldn't place it. She grinned and shook her head, knowing the earworm song was going to create havoc inside her head trying to come up with the song's name.

A few minutes later, the police officer brought Iris into the room. She wasn't a big girl. Far from it. 5'2 and weighing in at about one hundred pounds. She was twenty-one years old but looked like a teenager.

"Are you okay?" Dana asked.

"I'm fine," Iris said, chewing on a nail. She didn't look fine, but why would she? She was jailed in a foreign country thousands of miles from her home country of Sweden.

"Jeez, Iris, what did you get yourself mixed up in?" Dana asked.

Iris began to cry.

"I just want to go back home now to Sweden," she said. "Please don't press charges against me. I didn't mean you any harm."

"You broke into my home at two in the morning. It was terrifying."

"I know. I'm sorry. I was so stupid."

"I'm not going to argue with you about that," Dana said.

She watched a demure Iris for a moment then looked at Benny, who shrugged his shoulders.

"Listen, Iris," Dana said, leaning in close to the Swede. "I'm not looking to jam you up worse than you already are here. But if you want to go home sooner rather than later, then tell me everything you know about those darn orchids and why you would risk exactly this," Dana said with her hands in the air to show she meant the jail.

Iris looked up at Dana with more tears welling up in her eyes.

"I... I want to help," she said, her voice quivering.

"Okay, then let's start from the beginning. We want to hear every detail of how you went from biodiversity student to being arrested for breaking and entering in the span of mere days.

And I mean it when I say I want to hear every detail. Every. Single. Detail."

Iris took in a big breath. "Okay," she said as she breathed out. "I'll tell you everything."

# CHAPTER TWENTY-FIVE

DANA HAD ASKED IRIS TO TELL HER EVERYTHING SHE KNEW, and she did just that. She started from her arrival at the reserve until the night Max Perry drove her to Casa Verde. He gave her one of the reserve's blankets—which proved to be the proverbial nail in her coffin from a legal perspective.

Iris had told them her story from the begining. She began to see Perry romantically within a week of her arrival at the reserve. Two weeks after that, she was in love with the handsome scientist.

Iris explained how it felt like she was under a spell with him, that only after being arrested did it begin to break its hold over her.

She told Dana and Benny how Perry had convinced her that the orchids could and should only remain on the land where they had chosen to grow. He had convinced her that in the wrong hands, the orchids were doomed. They couldn't let a simpleton like Ramón take those orchids away and do who knows what to them.

So Perry drove Iris down from the reserve to Mariposa Beach. It was 1:45 a.m. when he parked near Casa Verde. He would wait for her while she climbed the wall and located the orchids in the greenhouse.

"Just do it like we practiced," he had told before handing her the green blanket from the reserve and sending her over the wall and onto Dana's property.

*What a scum bucket*, Dana kept thinking as Iris told them her story.

"So you went over that wall on your own?" Benny asked.

A thin grin crept on Iris's face for the first time. "I was a gymnast in school and a CrossFit nut," she said with pride.

"Remind me to beef up my security," Dana said to Benny.

"Once I was over the wall and on your property, I went straight to the greenhouse which Max had drawn up on a piece of paper he gave me. But it was so dark and I was so scared, I started to panic, and then I got turned around."

"That explains why I saw your flashlight prancing around in the dark like a forest fairy."

"Max had assured me everyone would be in bed sleeping, so I would be able to get in and out of there quickly."

"Unlucky for you, I couldn't sleep that night, so I went to get some fresh air on my balcony."

Iris bowed her head down. She sighed and continued. "I finally found the door to the greenhouse and was about to enter it when I heard that man shouting, then I saw a flashlight coming in my direction, so I just ran. All I heard was shouting and then what sounded like a loud firecracker, which terrified me because I realized it wasn't a firecracker but someone shooting at me. I was so scared that I cleared the wall easily with all that adrenaline surging through my body. But I was scared that I was sloppy. I left that stupid blanket behind."

"Along with a piece of your shirt and hair," Dana reminded her.

"Well, it was my first time being a criminal, and as you can see, I'm not very good at it."

"And you did all this because you thought you were saving the orchids? When that's all we're trying to do as well," Dana said.

"I don't think she did it just for the orchids," Benny said, sounding skeptical.

Tears welled up in Iris's eyes again. "I did it because Max asked me to. I love him."

*Oh brother*, Dana thought. She had watched enough *Locked Up Abroad* on National Geographic to know about women who are manipulated by their boyfriends to smuggle drugs from abroad into their home countries only to end up in jail somewhere in Peru or Mexico. She actually felt bad for the girl. She was young, dumb, and in love. Easy pickings for a master manipulator, and by the way Max Perry had played everyone, Dana was convinced he was just that.

It also put the murder of Doña Elsa's husband into a whole new light. Perhaps he had manipulated that whole scenario. Using Eladio's history of womanizing to get Doña Elsa to finally snap after decades of shoddy treatment and humiliation so that she killed her husband with Max Perry whispering in her ear the whole time, hoping she would do just that.

"So what's going to happen to me?" Iris asked.

Dana looked at Benny. "I don't know, but don't worry. You hopped over a wall. They're not going to lock you up and throw away the key," Dana said.

"Please, I'm begging you, don't press charges. I'll never do anything like this again. I'll be on the first flight back to Sweden and out of your life, I swear."

Iris's face and body demurred, reminding Dana of Puss in Boots in the Shrek movies when he's looking up at his foes with big, sad eyes. Dana couldn't help but feel that she was the one being manipulated now.

"We'll see," she said as she got up from the table and left the visiting room.

BENNY FOLLOWED DANA OUTSIDE, telling the guard they were done with the visit. He then had to play catch-up as Dana hastily made her way out to the parking lot.

"Hey, what's going on?" he asked her once they were outside of the police station.

"I don't like being played," she said.

"By whom? Iris?"

"By Iris and by Max."

"How so?"

"Well, this whole 'I'm so sorry act, please let me go' routine we just went through in there."

Benny scratched the back of his head. He was usually the skeptical one, believing the worst from people right off the bat— a nasty side effect of being in the legal profession for as long as he had been. But Dana was the opposite. She always gave people the benefit of the doubt. A huge believer in second chances. That's why she always seemed to be getting mixed up in these types of situations, because she cared too much about people. So this was a bit of a 180 from the Dana he knew and loved.

"Okay, well, sure, that is a possibility, but she sounded sincere," Benny said.

"I don't know. She twirls that blonde hair of hers and flutters those big, bright blue eyes of her. I think she has a lot of experience playing the good-girl card to get out of big trouble."

"You need to have a little bit more solid information to go by than that," Benny said, sounding like the lawyer he was.

Dana sighed and looked at him. "There is one thing that is bugging me and making me think what we just witnessed in there was one big show."

"I'm listening," Benny said when Dana stood there for a moment quietly.

"Max Perry has never been to Casa Verde. I've never talked to him about my property or that I have a greenhouse. So just how the heck did he know about the greenhouse? And not just know about it, but also know exactly where it was so that he could draw Iris a map? He would have no way of knowing that."

Benny stood there in shock. "You're right."

THE DRIVE back to Mariposa Beach from the police station in Nicoya was tense. Could Max Perry be innocent? Could he be the one that was being manipulated?

"Okay, so let's think of the suspects here," Dana said as she sat in the passenger side of Benny's SUV.

"Dana, we're not the police," Benny said.

He had suggested right there and then while they were in Nicoya, literally standing in front of the Judicial Police station, to march back inside and let the detectives know about the whole greenhouse location situation with Max Perry.

Dana didn't want to jump the gun. Besides, she knew Detectives Picado and Rojas were out looking to arrest Max Perry as the mastermind of the break-in, so if he was really the one behind it all like Iris said, then he would be sitting in jail soon enough.

"I know we're not the police, but let's think this through and make sure the right person is behind bars."

Benny mulled it over for a while. "Okay, I'll bite. But you're not going to like it."

Dana gave him a side-eye look.

"Don't even say it," she said.

"Hey, you're the one who wants to play police and come up with suspects," Benny said.

"Ramón would never be mixed up in anything like this," Dana said, sounding angry. "Besides, we already had the orchids in our possession. Why would he stage a break-in when he had direct access to them already? And I don't think he's ever even met Iris."

Benny furrowed his eyebrows at the valid points.

"I do need to talk to him right away, though," Dana said.

"About?"

"If anyone knows who would know about the location of the greenhouse, it would be Ramón."

THEY MADE it back to Casa Verde in record time. As Benny drove up the driveway, they could tell right away that something was amiss. Ramón's landscaping tools were strewn about, something he would never do. He took pride in keeping his work area neat and tidy, and he treated his tools like they were made out of gold.

Dana looked at Benny, and she could tell he was picking up on the bad vibe as well.

"I've never seen Ramón leave a mess like that behind," Dana said ominously.

"Me neither." Benny drove slowly as he pulled up to the front of the house. He maneuvered through the turnaround and back into the driveway.

"Planning a quick getaway," Dana said teasingly.

"From the looks of things, I thought it would be prudent."

He reached into the glove compartment and reached for his holstered Glock firearm for which he had all the legal papers for owning it and carrying it as a concealed weapon.

Dana looked at it nervously, but she was happy to be able to count on its protection. Part of her brain was telling her to get the heck out of Dodge, but she was worried about Ramón and Carmen and didn't want to leave without checking in on them.

"Let me call Ramón first," Dana said.

"Let's do it from inside the house. I feel like a sitting duck in the car. These transitional spaces are usually the most dangerous," Benny said.

Dana agreed and they exited the SUV carefully, looking around before beelining to the house. Dana had changed the locks to the house to one of those smart locks which turned into a keyless deadbolt, so she unlocked the door using a phone app before exiting the SUV and they quickly went inside and locked the door.

"I think we're getting too paranoid," Dana said, blowing hair strands from her face. It was just an old nervous habit, since she no longer had long hair, but she had found that when she got stressed, she would blow imaginary hair strands away.

"Better safe than sorry," Benny said.

Dana called Ramón. No answer. That was very strange, since usually Ramón or his wife were around to answer.

"Nothing. I'll try his cell phone," Dana said as she dialed it.

He didn't answer.

"He didn't pick up. I'm worried," Dana said as she fired off a text.

ARE YOU THERE, RAMÓN?

She stared at her phone, hoping to see those three dancing dots that indicated he was texting her back, but nothing. Then they heard a crashing sound from outside that made them both jump. They peered out the window towards the direction of the sound.

"That's coming from the greenhouse," Dana said. "I'm calling the police."

Costa Rica has a 911 service just like the United States, so Dana dialed 9-1-1. The dispatcher answered right away, and Dana reported that they believed there was an intruder in her property for the second time in three days. The dispatcher told her to stay put, not to go out and investigate. Police were on the way. But that meant at least fifteen to twenty minutes, unless Officer Freddy Sánchez happened to be patrolling or on a call close to Mariposa Beach.

"What if Ramón and Carmen are out there needing life-saving help?" Dana said.

Benny agreed. He pulled out his handgun from its holster.

"I'll go check out, you wait here," he said.

"I don't think so. This is my property they're messing with, and they're really ticking me off," Dana said as she went to the hallway closet and reached for her .22 rifle, which was still loaded from when Iris broke in.

Benny knew arguing was a moot point, so he just told her to be very careful.

"Does that really need to be said?" Dana said. He shrugged his shoulders and they headed outside.

"Ramón. Carmen," Dana called out as she walked right behind Benny slowly. She held the rifle in a low ready position. She wasn't the best shot in the world, and she told herself after this ordeal she was going to take lessons, because it seemed there wasn't a dull moment down here in the tropical paradise that is Mariposa Beach.

Dana fired a round up in the air like she had last night but neglected to let Benny know of her plans, causing him to jump in the air in fright.

"What are you doing?" he said, sounding angry and annoyed all at once.

"Sorry, figured I would fire a warning shot off," Dana said, knowing she had messed up.

"Warning shots are a waste of ammunition, so I wouldn't bother, but next time, warn me. You almost gave me a heart attack."

"Sorry," Dana said once again, then she giggled. She put her hand over her mouth to stop from laughing, emanating a bizarre snorting sound.

Benny gave her a *really, you're laughing* look. "Sorry," she said for a third time. "It's nervous laughter, can't help myself," she whispered.

They continued towards the greenhouse, and there were sure signs of a struggle, but they couldn't see anyone.

"Ramón, are you there?" Benny said as they slowly approached the greenhouse.

The door was ajar, so they peered inside and on the floor was Ramón lying unconscious.

"Oh no, Ramón," Dana said as she bolted inside.

"Dana, wait..." Benny said, but it was too late. She was inside, kneeling next to Ramón, who was out cold, bleeding from the head.

Benny looked around. Seeing no one, he went into the greenhouse.

"Is he..."

"No, thank God, he's breathing," Dana said, tearing up.

Benny looked around. "I don't see the orchids," he said.

Dana stood up and went to the corner of the greenhouse where Ramón had stored them. "They're gone. Unless he had already planted them, but he promised he would wait for me, since I wanted to see the process."

"I can't believe this is all happening over some orchids."

"I know, this is crazy. I never thought there would be orchids to die for," Dana said, shaking her head. "Oh my gosh, Carmen," Dana said as she and Benny made their way down to Ramón and Carmen's house. They found her inside, tied up, but alive.

OFFICER SÁNCHEZ ARRIVED ten minutes later. Ramón had regained consciousness. He was groggy but enraged that his attacker had manhandled his wife more than anything else.

"Did you recognize your attacker?" Sánchez asked.

"No. He wore a mask and didn't speak. I was working in the greenhouse, next thing I know I woke up on the floor. The orchids are gone."

"And that's all that was taken?" an incredulous Sánchez asked.

"I just looked around quickly, and that is all that appears to have been stolen. He didn't even try to break into the house," Dana said.

"Are you going up to the reserve?" Benny asked.

"There is a patrol unit on its way. The OIJ is also heading down from Nicoya," Sánchez said.

"It doesn't make sense for Max to do this. He has to know he would be prime suspect number one," Dana said.

"He might not be playing with a full deck, so his judgment is clouded," Benny said.

"Way clouded from the look of things. All this for some flowers?" Sánchez said.

"It seems like pharmaceutical companies would pay big bucks for them, so they could be worth a lot of money," Dana said.

"And easier to smuggle than drugs and much less of a punishment if caught," Benny added.

Sánchez nodded his head in agreement on that part. "That smuggler they arrested at the airport last week is already free," he said.

"Curt Bennett is out of jail?" Dana asked, shocked.

"Yes. Two days ago. The girl too," Sánchez said.

"What? Iris was freed?" Dana said.

"Yes. This afternoon."

Dana was shocked. "Hmm, so those two are cut loose and all heck breaks loose down here."

# CHAPTER TWENTY-SIX

Dana and Benny drove up to the reserve. Ramón wanted to come along, but he was still a bit wobbly on his feet thanks to the concussion he received when the intruder snuck up on him from behind and whacked him on the top of his head with a clay flower pot. Carmen had also been adamant. He was staying put. The police suspected Max Perry was behind all the havoc, and he was MIA, so she didn't want Ramón outside of Casa Verde. She figured since the cursed orchids were gone, Perry wouldn't be back to Casa Verde, so he was staying put. The OIJ had an all-out-points bulletin and were monitoring both international airports in the country.

Dana was meeting up with Claro Madderra, who had asked her to come up to discuss everything that had been going on the past few days and about how to arrange another trip down to the part of the reserve where the rare orchids grew so they could try it again. That's what she wanted to work out with him the most. To heck with everything else. If the pharma companies stole the orchids so they could make millions off anti-aging creams, then so be it. At least the orchids would still be protected in the wild right in Casa Verde.

She knew the easy thing to do would be for her to throw her hands in the air and give up, saying *well, I tried*. But she wasn't one to be intimidated into backing down from just about anything—much to Benny's chagrin.

Dana figured it was the old journalist spirit inside of her that arose in these types of situations where she became eager to fight for what is right and hold those in power in check. At least that's what old-school journalism used to be all about. That type of reporting is harder to come by now in the current landscape of instant 24/7 news, where even the mainstream media competes for eyeballs, so they have to get down in the mud with all the other outlets out there—legit and otherwise—to fight for those online clicks to justify their existence to adversities.

Then again, perhaps, as her mother liked to remind her, she was just stubborn like a mule. Had been that way since before she could crawl, her mom would tease her.

During the drive up to the reserve, Dana called Detective Gabriela Rojas to see if there were new developments. It had been less than twenty-four hours, but how hard could it be to find an American like Max Perry trying to hide in such a small country?

"You would be surprised," Benny had told her. "A lot of tax cheats come down to hide in Costa Rica, and that's with the IRS hot to trot in comparison to the USDA after a possible plant smuggler."

Dana figured there was a lot of truth to that. If the item everyone was after were something like cocaine versus orchids, then the authorities in Costa Rica and the United States would be more eager to track down Max Perry and they wouldn't have let Curt Bennett out of jail to roam the country free as a bird.

She also wondered if Iris had gone back to the reserve. Rojas explained since Dana hadn't filed the paperwork to report Iris's crime of breaking into her property and the crime was a lowly misdemeanor by someone with a clean record, that Picado cut her loose a little bit earlier than necessary. You cannot be held in detention longer than twenty-four hours without a court order. She was released after fifteen hours in custody.

"So you think she went back to the reserve?" Benny asked as she drove.

"Where else could she go? She's been staying in the reserve's student dorms since she arrived in the country, and her stuff is there."

"If I were her, I would head out to the airport post haste and get the heck out of town," Benny said.

"Maybe she's halfway to Sweden as we speak," Dana said.

Claro greeted them at the front gate and escorted them to the main building.

"Did Iris come back here?" Dana asked.

Claro nodded his head. "She didn't have anywhere to go, so I told her she could stay here, but only for two nights. That is more than enough time for her to find someplace to stay or make the necessary travel arrangements to go back to Sweden."

"Is she here now? I would like to talk to her," Dana said.

"No. She went into town to find other living arrangements."

"I wonder if she's meeting up with Max," Dana said.

"It would be foolish of them to try and get together, since I would imagine the police have a tail on her. Probably why they released her, hoping she would lead them straight to Max Perry," Claro said.

"You haven't seen that Curt Bennett guy hanging around here?" Dana asked.

"No, I've never seen him before, until that email you sent me with his photograph."

"Well, that's all a matter for the police," Benny said.

Dana smiled. "Okay, party pooper. So Claro, can we

arrange to have Ramón come back up here so we can give it another go of moving those orchids to Casa Verde?"

"Sure. But give me a few days. Everything is hectic right now with this Iris and Max situation and the missing orchids. The police coming and going. I don't want to do anything to kick the hornet's nest. Once things settle down, we can get back to the business of saving those orchids from Forever Young," Claro said.

"Oh, you've heard of the Forever Young Corporation?" Dana said.

Claro seemed flustered for a moment before smiling wide again. "Well, they've been pestering Doña Elsa nonstop about getting a footing into the reserve so they could get their hands on those orchids, so I just assumed they're somehow in the picture in this big old mess."

Dana smiled. "Okay, sounds good. I'll reach out to you next week and figure out when Ramón and I can come back out here." She turned to Benny. "Let's go, hon."

"Sounds good," Claro said.

Dana and Benny were almost at the door when Curt Bennett came out of one of the offices which had its door closed.

He gave them a hard stare and he was holding a gun.

# CHAPTER TWENTY-SEVEN

"Over there. Back to where you came from," Bennett said as he waved the pistol around.

Dana turned to Claro for help.

"What are you doing, Curt? I had this all under control," Claro said.

Dana felt like a balloon whose air was slowly being let out by a giggling child.

"You must have blinders on, because that's not how I'm seeing things," Bennett said. He turned his attention to Benny. "You put that gun you have in that back holster on the floor and kick it over to me. Now."

Dana looked at Benny, who looked deflated. A poker player with a fat stack of chips losing them all in the final hand. Dana figured Curt was the one who attacked Ramón and Carmen at Casa Verde and saw Benny with his gun, so he knew he had one.

Benny did as ordered. Curt picked up Benny's gun from the floor while keeping his own gun pointed at Dana and Benny. He handed the gun to Claro.

Claro took the gun and said, "It was all under control." This time he seethed as he said it.

"I haven't gone through all this monkey business to miss out on the gold medal right at the finishing line," Bennett said.

"What is going on?" a flustered Benny said.

"These two have been in cahoots the whole time," Dana said. "I let Claro's friendship with Doña Elsa and Ramón cloud my better judgment."

"Friendship? Ramón is a peasant. Doña Elsa? She treats me like I'm her peasant. Doing all the backbreaking work around here and for what? Pennies," Claro said. His friendly demeanor and voice were gone, replaced by bitter eyes and an angry cadence.

"The reserve is a nonprofit. What did you expect?" Dana said as Benny gave her arm a gentle squeeze as if to implore her to not kick the hornet's nest.

"I expected when there was a chance for everyone to make a lot of money from just selling the rights to a few stupid orchids that she wouldn't be so pigheaded as to say no to all that money. Easy for her to take the moral high ground when she's raking in thousands of dollars a day in donations from her Facebook group alone. And she gets to be the big hero. Doing the right thing for the plants and the wildlife. Well, what about human life? What about me?"

"If you were in trouble financially, I'm sure she would have helped you," Dana said.

"I'm not getting down to my hands and knees to beg her for a darn thing. I've earned it. I'm the one who built this place up, not her," Claro said.

Dana could now feel the hatred and contempt he had been bottling up deep inside for who knows how long. It just dawned on her that he didn't care for Elsa, far from that. He hated her.

"Oh gosh, Claro, what did you do to get Doña Elsa imprisoned? You killed Eladio," Dana said.

He puffed out his chest proudly, realizing that Dana had just figured out his role behind that. "I needed both Doña Elsa and that idiot of her husband out of my way. So I killed two birds with one stone, and all I had to do was kill Don Eladio and make sure she got all the credit so she could rot in prison," Claro said proudly.

"But why?" Benny asked.

Dana answered. "Why give away the goose that lays those golden eggs when all he had to do was get rid of Doña Elsa and Eladio and then he would ensure he would take over ownership of the reserve. So he killed Eladio and framed Doña Elsa."

"Bravo," he said.

"But that's preposterous," Benny said. "Their children stand to inherit, not him."

"I already have all the paperwork in place to declare this an official public wildlife reserve thanks to a buddy in the municipality, putting me in charge. For the better good of the community, of course. And all it cost me was ten thousand dollars."

"Didn't cost you ten thousand dollars. It cost me ten thousand dollars. Plus all the money I've put into all you idiots mucking things up for me. So let's get on with it. I'm not leaving until my ROI is secure," Bennett interrupted.

"So what's the big plan now, Claro? Kill us? What about Max and Iris? Are you going to kill them too?"

Claro laughed. "Just come on out," he said.

A smiling Iris came out of the office.

"You too, Max."

And out came a downtrodden-looking Max Perry.

"Feels like I'm at the circus. How many more clowns are going to come piling out of that small room?" Dana said.

"So you're all in this together," a disgusted-sounding Benny said.

"Everyone gets some of that pharma money. Claro also ends up with the land. And Max and Iris live happily ever after," Dana said.

Iris laughed. "You're half right," she said as she walked up to Claro and planted a big kiss on his lips.

"Well, I didn't see that coming. You got me there," Dana said.

"I'm sorry, Dana. I'm drowning in student debt. I need the money, so when Claro approached me, it made sense. What's the harm in selling those orchids to Forever Young? The people want these products that stop wrinkles and make people look younger. What's the harm? But Doña Elsa wouldn't budge, so they came to me. And I swear, I had no idea there would be violence."

"So now you're going to kill me, Benny, then Ramón and Carmen. You'll get rid of anyone that knows about the orchids and your dirty secrets," Dana said.

"That's right. We've come this far. Might as well cross the finish line," Claro said.

"And all this death and destruction for just a little bit of money," Dana said.

"Oh no, you're way, way off... it's a lot of stinking money," Claro said as he broke out in laughter.

"Okay, let's get on with it," Bennett snapped.

"Not here. I don't want to make a mess inside. Take them out back," Claro said.

Claro and Bennett walked Dana and Benny out the back door to the back of the building. It was wooded. The entire staff had been laid off, and all the other students were long gone, so there wasn't anyone else around. The reserve was in the middle of nowhere, without any neighbors for miles and miles. Dana could scream until she turned blue in the face and no one would hear her. No one would come to her rescue.

She held onto Benny's hand. He squeezed back tightly and kissed the top of her hand.

She felt horrible. It was all her fault. She was the one who got into the middle of these situations with these terrible people, and now she was going to cost Benny his life along with hers. But at least she had a little comfort, dying with a man that she had fallen in love with wholeheartedly.

"Come on, let's go," Bennet barked.

"I'm some journalist, aren't I?" she spoke softly to Benny. "I didn't see any of this coming."

"Neither did I. Evil usually blindsides good people like you," Benny said.

"And you. You're the kindest man I've met. You have such a big heart. Sorry I got you into this mess."

"You have nothing to apologize for. I love you, Dana."

"I love you, Benny."

"Yeah, yeah, yeah, how sweet," Bennett seethed.

Dana looked into Bennett's eyes and saw darkness.

Perry stood by the door, his eyes welled up with tears. "I can't watch this," he said, turning to go back inside.

Iris was standing next to him. "What a wuss," she said as she smiled and blew Claro a kiss.

Claro and Bennett stood in front of Dana and Benny with guns in their hands.

"Turn around. Both of you. Now," Bennett ordered.

Dana and Benny did as ordered. It was strange, Dana thought. She always wondered when she watched true crime shows or even a movie why people would obey someone whom they knew were going to kill them if they did what they told them to do.

*I would run, make it harder on them to kill me*, she would

think. And yet in real life there she was, doing as she was told. Frozen like a statue. But she felt at ease. Calm. She was holding Benny's hand and figured that had something to do with it. She felt love and was ready for whatever evil Claro and Bennett were about to do. She knew she and Benny were at peace. She closed her eyes and prayed while she waited for it.

What she heard was the loud sound of a whirring engine that oddly sounded like a lawnmower. Then she heard Iris yell, "Watch out, Claro." And then the sound of a large impact and the voices of Claro and Bennett screaming in pain.

# EPILOGUE

*A Week Later.*

"I needed this," Dana said. She and Benny were at a couple's massage at the Four Seasons Resort, which was about three hours away from Mariposa Beach in the Papagayo Peninsula. The resort was in the mountains, offering panoramic views of the Pacific.

It was quite the pampering. Full-body massages then a mud bath in a private cabana overlooking the Pacific Ocean. A bottle of Veuve Clicquot Yellow Label Brut champagne and fresh strawberries.

Claudio Villalobos, who was Ramón and Carmen's son, was the Assistant General Manager and he set everything up for them. He hooked them up VIP style.

"You'll be treated to the George and Amal Clooney experience," he had promised them, and he had delivered.

Dana had insisted it wasn't necessary; she and Benny just wanted to relax away from Mariposa Beach for a few days after spending a week dealing with the fallout at the wildflower reserve incident.

The police had told him how Bennett and Claro were planning to kill his parents after getting rid of Dana and Benny, so Claudio was grateful and wanted to thank them.

For Dana, if anyone should get thanked, it would be Max Perry, who at the last minute decided he couldn't be part to all that death, so he slipped away unnoticed and jumped onto Claro's black Yamaha ATV, which he used to charge towards Claro and Bennett like a bull towards the red flag.

Both men had their arms stretched out with guns in hand, about to execute Dana and Benny like they were mobsters in *The Godfather*. They weren't paying attention to what was coming towards them from their left side until it was too late.

Dana had told Claudio if it wasn't for Perry, she and Benny wouldn't be here either, but he didn't care. He gave her all the credit for saving his parents from being killed by that duo, so here they were getting the celebrity treatment at one of Costa Rica's swankiest resorts. The fact that the resort was Gustavo Barca's main competitor in the Guanacaste Province made it even sweeter for Dana. *I know, so petty,* she would say to herself when that thought crept in her head.

Perry drove that ATV into their would-be killers at full throttle. Both men lived, but they suffered multiple broken bones, including breaking so many ribs that Dana was surprised, not realizing how many ribs are in the human body.

By the time Perry had run them over and Dana turned around at the commotion, she caught a brief glimpse as both men came crashing to the ground like rag dolls.

Iris was beside herself in grief and anger over her beloved Claro lying on the ground all broken and spent, hardly conscious. Benny quickly grabbed one of the guns from the ground and subdued Iris by locking her inside the supply room until police arrived.

Perry was shaken, but he didn't know what else to do. He

had misgivings of getting involved with the likes of Bennett and Claro, but he did it for the money, although not at the expense of people's lives. He had no idea that Claro had killed Doña Elsa's husband so he could frame her for his murder until he had heard his confession. And he wanted no part in the murder of four more people.

The police arrived at the reserve and arrested Iris and Perry. Claro and Bennett were also under arrest, but due to their medical condition, they would have to wait until a pair of ambulances came all the way from Nosara to bring them to the hospital. They stayed there under arrest for five days until finally they were stable enough to be transferred to the prison infirmary in San José. Eventually they would be tried for the murder of Eladio Calderón and the attempted murder of Dana and Benny, as well as for conspiring to murder and for the aggravated assault of Ramón and Carmen. The two men also faced a litany of financial crimes and breaking and entering into Casa Verde. They were looking at decades behind bars.

Iris Kjellberg was charged as an accessory to all those crimes, and she wouldn't be able to twirl her blonde hair and flutter those blue eyes out of those charges. Benny figured she would serve a few years in prison depending on how much she was willing to cooperate with authorities, then she would be deported back to Sweden.

Detective Rojas told Dana that the prosecutor cut a deal with Perry, who would be their star witness. He would probably spend a few months in jail during the trials of the others and then be deported to the United States.

Dana thought that was fair. He got in well over his head with some very bad people that tricked a lot of people into thinking they were decent human beings. He would suffer further as a free man. His life as a scientist was over. He had already been expelled from the Ph.D. program at the University of Hawaii. A news report Dana had read indicated that the closest Max Perry could get to plants and trees as a professional would be mowing someone's yard.

Doña Elsa was immediately released from jail with the apology of the court and the Judicial Police. The reserve was back in her good hands. Her name cleared, the donations began to pour in so she could get the reserve going once again.

The first thing she did was hire back her laid-off staff. She was taking calls from all the schools that had dropped her, offering their apologies and their eagerness to get their student-exchange programs back on track. She was even getting calls from new schools who had found out about the great work she did and who were eager to form partnerships with her.

She was also getting a lot of attention from Hollywood and book publishers who smelled a juicy story of how she dealt with these lowlifes that were circling around her orchids like sharks to chum. Dana had connected Doña Elsa with an agent she knew in LA to help her deal with a different type of shark that's found circling around Hollywood: the studio executive.

"OH, THIS IS HEAVEN," Dana said as they sat in a steam room covered in mud with glasses of champagne nearby.

It was funny how almost dying together can bring a couple even closer. Not that she would offer that up as relationship advice to anyone. But she felt even closer to Benny than ever before, and they had even begun to talk about taking their relationship to the next level, something she would have never imagined she would consider after her divorce and her fleeing San Francisco for a new start in the tropical paradise that is Mariposa Beach. But she wasn't going to fight those feelings anymore. She moved down there to start over fresh, and that is just what she had done, and was now happy to let her new life take her where it wanted to go. She wasn't going to fight it anymore.

She looked over at Benny and smiled. "I love you," she said.

"I love you too," he said.

They then exchanged a muddy kiss as the steam room kicked into high gear, spraying them with hot water as the caked-on mud began to wash off their bodies, making them laugh out loud. They turned to look at the stunning sunset view over the Pacific. They held hands as they watched the sun slowly drop into the Pacific Ocean.

# ABOUT THE AUTHOR

I was born and raised in Costa Rica, but now live in San Francisco, California. I've always loved cozy mysteries, so when I decided to write one, I just knew I had to base it in my home country of Costa Rica!

That's how this beach cozy mystery series came about. I'm excited to bring you more cozy mysteries set in the Pacific Coast of Costa Rica.

You can learn more about me and my books over at my website: www.KCAmes.com.

Sign up for my newsletter for book updates, animal pics, and my recipe book of traditional Costa Rica dishes, for free:

kcames.com/subscribe

Find me online and say hello...